"That there's one fine buck," Johnna whispered.

Brows lifted, Laurel asked, "Which one?"

April tossed an apple into Laurel's lap and giggled. "Ours are all good, but only one of those men over at the table is. . . dreamy."

"Oh, no, April." Laurel shook her forefinger at her cousin. "You did this same thing when Eric arrived in Reliable Township. You mooned over him and all we heard was 'Dr. Walcott this' and 'Dr. Walcott that.' I'm saying here and now, you're not going to make a ninny of yourself just because a handsome man stumbled into our camp."

"So you think he's handsome, do you?" Kate gave Laurel a triumphant look.

"The real beauty of a person is on the inside. We know nothing about him," Laurel said primly, then quickly took another bite so she wouldn't be expected to say anything more.

CATHY MARIE HAKE is a Southern California native who loves her work as a nurse and Lamaze teacher. She and her husband have a daughter, a son, and two dogs, so life is never dull or quiet. Cathy considers herself a sentimental packrat, collecting antiques and Hummel figurines. In spare moments, she reads, bargain hunts, and makes a huge mess with her new hobby of scrapbooking.

Books by Cathy Marie Hake

Bridal Veil

Cathy Marie Hake

Heartsong Presents

A note from the Author:
I love to hear from my readers! You may correspond with me by writing:

Cathy Marie Hake
Author Relations
PO Box 721
Uhrichsville, OH 44683

ISBN 1-59310-869-9

BRIDAL VEIL

All scripture quotations are taken from the King James Version of the Bible.

All of the characters and events in this book are fictitious. Any resemblance to actual persons, living or dead, or to actual events is purely coincidental.

Our mission is to publish and distribute inspirational products offering exceptional value and biblical encouragement to the masses.

PRINTED IN THE U.S.A.

one

1891
Chance Ranch, outside of San Francisco

"It'll be such an adventure!" Paxton Chance could barely sit still. He looked across the table. "I've been reading all about Yosemite."

"I'm going, too," Caleb declared.

"Me, three." Calvin didn't even swallow his bite of ham before inviting himself along.

Laurel Chance didn't think for a single moment that this trip was a spur-of-the-moment whim. For weeks, ever since the local paper had featured an article about the newly created national park, her brothers and cousins had been hatching the plan.

"What about your responsibilities around here?" Laurel's dad asked.

"We've got it all worked out. Half of us Chances will go and so will half of the MacPhersons. Then we'll come back and trade off with the ones who stayed here."

"I wanna go with the first group," eleven-year-old Percy declared as he grabbed the bowl of mashed potatoes and *thwapped* a huge dollop onto his plate.

The older Chance boys exchanged a pained glance.

"Now hold on a second." Her uncle Gideon looked at his younger son. "According to my thinking, you have something else you're to do this summer."

Percy jolted, and his scrawny chest puffed out.

Uncle Gideon nodded sagely. "Your mother and I discussed

it last night. Time's come for you to train your horse, Son."

"What about me?"

"And me?"

Laurel stiffened. One of the things she loved most about home was the reliability of life on Chance Ranch. Year in and year out, life went according to the same timetable, the same ebb and flow. Suddenly, that had changed. The older boys wanted to hie off, and the younger ones were being promised horses now instead of having to wait until they reached the age of twelve. *What's happening here?*

Uncle Bryce thumped his hand on the table. "Listen up. We took a vote last night."

"You took a vote?" Caleb looked thunderstruck. "Without me?"

Uncle Gideon stood to speak. Everyone fell silent.

"You kids have done us all proud. It'd be nice for you to all have a grand adventure to look back on later in life, and Yosemite sounds like just the place. We did a lot of thinking and praying, so here's what we've decided."

Laurel watched her cousins all lean forward. It wasn't until she glanced to the side that she realized Kate and April were holding their breath, too. *They want to go!* The very idea stunned her.

All of this talk about adventure made no sense to Laurel. She didn't desire to take a big journey and felt no need to have exploits to recall in her dotage. Ordinary life pleased her; she found contentment in the everydayness of Chance Ranch. The very thought of her cousins wanting to do this—well, she could chalk that up to what Aunt Lovejoy termed, "Male sap flowing through young veins." But for the girls to go? Ridiculous!

"Now this plan comes with a commitment." Uncle Gideon stared directly at Caleb.

Caleb's eyes narrowed. "I'm twenty-one, and you left me

out of the vote. Now I see why."

Uncle Gideon continued as if his son hadn't said a thing. "It's a two-year plan. This year, the eight oldest boys all go for seven weeks. Yes, all of you. While you're gone, the rest of us will hold down the ranch. The next four boys in line are getting horses."

"Me, too?" Cory croaked.

Uncle Gideon nodded. "We're expecting you juniors to become men a little early, and you'll have to prove yourselves. Any slacking or whining, and you'll forfeit the horse and have to wait two more years.

"We've designed the plan so when summer rolls around in 1892, those of you who go this year will stay behind and let the rest of us go explore."

Caleb's jaw hardened. "What all this boils down to is you're asking me not to make any promises to Greta."

"Not exactly. If you and Greta pray about it and find you're ready to marry, we'll grant you our blessing to become betrothed. No marrying up until the autumn after we return."

"I want to go this year," April said.

Tobias and Tanner both groaned.

Kate folded her arms across her chest. "Just what do you think you guys are going to do about eating if we girls don't come?"

"You and April, maybe." Calvin shot a look at Laurel. His scowl darkened. "But Miss Priss? No thanks."

Ouch! His attitude stung. Laurel gave him an outraged look. He motioned for her to pass the corn bread.

Looking down at her plate, Laurel pretended she hadn't seen him gesture. *He has a lot of nerve, asking for the corn bread I made after insulting me like that!*

"No kidding," Caleb tacked on. "The last thing we want is to have Laurel fussing about getting freckles or shrieking when she spies a snake."

"All the girls go together," Aunt Alisa declared.

"Only if they all want to go, right?" Tanner's voice still held hope.

"Only if they want to go," Uncle Titus agreed.

Kate looked at her parents, then at April and Laurel. "We're not letting this opportunity slip past us, are we?"

"Absolutely not! Count me in." April slathered honey on a chunk of corn bread. To Laurel's dismay, April then caught Cal's gesture and passed him the platter of corn bread.

It would serve him right to choke on it. Laurel stunned herself with that uncharitable thought. But still, the way the boys were talking about her hurt. Everyone on Chance Ranch was accepted and teased; nevertheless, this teasing was sharp as barbed wire. The boys truly didn't want her to go along, and they weren't sparing her feelings in the least.

"Just a minute." Caleb rapped his knuckles on the tabletop. "We're not staying at one of those log cabins or fancy hotels. This is tent camping. It'll be rough"—he gave Laurel a piercing look and tacked on—"*real* rough."

"They have hotels?" Laurel asked. Maybe they could compromise.

"We're going to be miles from them," one of her cousins informed her in a tone tinged with victory.

April shrugged. "Who cares? We want to go do something different. A tent sounds fun. I'll take care of packing up all the kitchen gear and determining a menu and food supplies."

"Then it's settled." Kate grinned at Laurel. "I know you wouldn't hold us back. It's all for one and one for all."

"Oh, man." Tanner slapped his hand on his forehead. "They're just like the Three Musketeers in petticoats."

Male snickers and guffaws resonated in the yard.

"The other two girls can go." Mom patted Laurel's hand. "Sweetheart, if you'd rather not make the trip, you're under no obligation."

"She wouldn't dare go," one of the boys muttered. "It'll ruin it for us all."

Thoroughly nettled by that attitude, Laurel lifted her chin. "Of course, I'm going. I wouldn't miss this trip for all the tea in China."

"Oh, boy, and she'll probably pack all that tea and china," Cal grumbled.

Laurel pasted a smile on her face, batted her lashes, and said, "You'll be invited to eat off that china, so don't complain." Deep inside, though, she cringed. *I just let my temper lead me into folly.*

❧

Gabriel Rutlidge halted a foot from the ledge and scanned the vista before him. A crisp breeze cut through his shirtsleeves and leather vest, cooling him after the exertion of the climb. The air smelled of a heady mix of pine, but an updraft carried hints of cedar and sequoia. A hawk rode the unseen air stream.

Majestic. No other word described Yosemite. Gabe absorbed the beauty spread before him and knew a sense of satisfaction that this land would be left unspoiled. He'd come here with the sole intent of appreciating nature at its finest and exploring the vast expanses of land now designated as the nation's preserve. Reports hadn't begun to prepare him for what he'd encountered.

"Hey, Rutlidge!"

Gabe shaded his eyes as he turned. He'd heard the horses coming but hoped the riders would turn the other direction and miss him. "What?"

"You didn't check in," one of the soldiers called to him. "Cap'n's hot under the collar."

"Tell the captain I have a mother back in Boston. I don't need anyone else worrying about me."

The three soldiers chortled, but they didn't depart. One kneed his bay and approached.

"We just went through an area south of the big meadow.

There's talk of clearing a footpath to some of the rock faces and falls."

Gabe stood silently and shook his head.

"It's going to be done. You know it will. Cap'n said we might as well plot the routes to minimize the impact. You were so opinionated about the last map, he reckoned you might want to weigh in before things get finalized."

"Fine. Where's your camp?"

The soldier shot him a cocky smile. "Found yours. Cap'n's waitin'."

Amused, Gabe lifted his canteen in a silent toast, then took a refreshing gulp of the water he'd fetched from a bubbling stream earlier that day. "Let me guess. The captain's making himself at home, and his cook just raided my supplies."

"Didn't stay long enough to answer that supposition, sir."

Another soldier leaned forward and patted his horse. "It'd please my belly iff'n you'd head back down, Mr. Rutledge. From the looks of what you had hanging in the branches, I'm shore the cook'll be happy to fix us up something fine."

"Go on ahead. Just save some for me." Gabe sat down. "I want to savor the view awhile."

"Don't wait too long, sir. I don't need to tell you, when night falls, it falls fast up here."

Smiling wryly, Gabe agreed, "You don't need to tell me. Keep fretting like that, Sergeant, and I'll think you're hoping to make captain soon."

The men rode off, and Gabe turned the other way. Though he hadn't said so, he'd welcome some companionship at supper. He and the buffalo soldiers had an unspoken agreement—they informally checked in and shared supplies as necessary. When they—or he—ran short of supplies, they shared so restocking only took place when it became absolutely essential.

In an area this vast and wild, it only made sense to have an emergency plan. Gabe knew he'd been remiss in not checking in. Undoubtedly, the captain would make his displeasure clear by helping himself to something especially toothsome from the supplies. *Fine by me,* he thought. He couldn't claim any great culinary skill. Simply searing meat, eating jerked beef, or opening cans was all Gabe could do. A good, hot meal and camaraderie around the fire would suit him for a night or two—long enough for him to set out plans for the next week or so. Then he'd be on his own again.

Yes, this was why he'd come—to explore, to have time to appreciate nature, and not be bothered by trifling details and petty grievances. He'd left that all behind him five years ago and never once regretted the decision.

This is where I belong. A place as untamed and spirited as I am—and it goes on and on forever. He stretched his arms wide. Wind blew through his hair and left him with the elated feeling of soaring free.

two

"Here, honey." Mama handed Laurel a package.

"Thank you, Mama." Laurel shook her head. "You've already been so generous. I can't imagine another thing—"

"Open it up," Daddy urged.

The brown paper rustled as Laurel carefully unwrapped it. She caught her breath. "Oh!"

"Your daddy bought that for you in San Francisco the last time he delivered my paintings to the gallery," Mama said. "Look."

Laurel watched as her mother and father twisted a wooden bar and opened a collapsible easel.

"It's surprisingly sturdy, even though it's compact." Daddy smoothed his big, rough hand over the frame. "I'm looking forward to seeing what you create on it."

"I'll be sure to make a picture especially for you. Thank you so much!" She hugged her parents.

"I think you're taking more art supplies than clothes," Daddy teased.

Laurel grinned. "I wasn't very keen on the idea of this trip at first, but when I realized what beautiful scenery I'd have to paint and draw, we couldn't leave fast enough."

"I helped her pack. She's taking plenty of clothes," Mama declared.

"I'm not sure that'll matter," Laurel said. "After the first day on the trip, anyone will undoubtedly mistake us all for being grubby urchins. The girls and I packed plenty of soap, but I'm not sure we'll be able to bully the boys into using it."

Paxton shot her a grimace. "It's biblical. Adam was made

from the dust of the earth. I don't know why you women are always trying to force us to go against our nature. Cowboys out on the trail live in the same set of clothes for weeks on end. Nothing's wrong with just living with the clothes on my back."

"That," Mama said crisply, "is why I insisted on packing for you."

Pax waited until Daddy folded down the easel and pressed it into Laurel's trunk. Once the lid was latched, Pax hefted the huge steamer trunk, let out a theatrical moan, and lugged it out of the girls' cabin. Laurel heard him muttering about it weighing down the wagon so much, they'd never catch up with the others in their group.

"I think he's still sore that you didn't let him go on to the fort to deliver the horses," Laurel whispered.

"You're more precious than a string of horses," Mama said. "Besides, he's made that delivery other times and will again in the future."

"Chances protect their women above all else," Daddy stated firmly. "Tobias, Pax, and Caleb are our strongest. Teaming them along with Peter and Ulysses MacPherson gives me reassurance that our girls will be okay."

"I'm sure we'll all be fine," Laurel said. She didn't want her father to have any last-minute misgivings and keep her from going.

"It did the other boys good to go without the eldest ones leading them," Daddy mused. "This gives Cal and Tanner an opportunity to assert themselves. Our decisions about this whole affair were prayed over—we want this to be fun, but it needs to allow everyone to do some maturing."

Laurel nodded. "Without the adults, everyone is going to have to grow up some. I'll keep watch over them for you all."

Her parents exchanged a look and nodded.

Caleb came lumbering in. "Sis said she forgot something.

Can't for the life of me fathom what. She's packed every last thing she owns."

"What was it?"

Caleb scowled. "Something stupid. I forget." He looked around. "What's left?"

Laurel didn't laugh or tease him. It would be stupid. They had to travel together for the next several days.

"Oh." Caleb colored deeply. He glanced up at the sleeping loft.

Laurel guessed at once. "I'll take care of that." She couldn't imagine Caleb scrambling up the ladder and coming back down with his sister's ruffled nightgown.

"Thanks." Caleb beat a hasty retreat. Laurel shimmied up the ladder.

"Check under Kate's pillow, too," Mama called up. "If April forgot her gown, Kate probably did, too."

"You're right," Laurel called down as she found both of them.

"Drop the gowns down. I'll stuff them in a sugar sack so the boys won't gawk at them."

"I had my reservations about allowing you girls to live together here in this cabin." Daddy chuckled. "But times like this, I can see why it was a good idea."

Laurel came back down and gave him a hug. "It was a grand idea. I'll keep careful watch on the girls while we're gone."

"We'll never get there if you won't leave," Ulysses MacPherson grumbled from the doorway.

Laurel laughed at his comment. Ulysses and Peter MacPherson sort of invited themselves along on the trip, and the girls promptly invited Johnna as well. The rest of the MacPherson clan would undoubtedly help out the Chances the next two summers, but that help would be returned in the following two when they planned to go to Yosemite. They weren't just neighbors; they were distant relatives through Aunt

Lovejoy. As "kissin' cousins," the children of both families always did things together.

"You're the last one to have her trunk packed," Johnna commented from the doorway. "I've been packed for days."

Mama spread her arms, and Johnna dashed over for a hug. Laurel wrapped her arms around both of them. "I'm so glad you're coming along."

"Me, too!" Johnna said.

As they all separated, Mama nodded, "So am I!"

Eyes sparkling with enthusiasm, Johnna promised, "I'll help Laurel keep tight rein on Kate and April."

Mama grabbed Laurel and gave her one last tight hug, whispering, "You be careful."

"Yes, Mama." Laurel pulled away. "I love you, too."

"Then here are the girl's nightgowns." Mama handed her the sugar sack.

Johnna let out a sound of dismay. "Oh, no!"

"So much for packing early," Laurel teased. "Don't worry. I have an extra." Carefully keeping her back to Ulysses to block his view of her lingerie, she opened a drawer and added one last flannel garment to the sugar sack. "I'm ready. Let's go!"

"We could have been most of the way there by now if you girls weren't intent on totin' along half of your worldly belongings," Ulysses ribbed.

"You'd do well to hope we packed the right half," Laurel said. "And when you see how much food April is taking, you won't grumble another word."

They all walked toward the four wagons. Ulysses took the sack and shoved it into a less-packed spot and informed Laurel, "Food is essential."

She smiled sweetly at him. "And just think: Since our party has four women, we'll be allowed some firearms. Otherwise, as soon as you entered Yosemite, the cavalry would confiscate your sidearms."

Peter steered April and Kate to the nearest wagon. "I, for one, am glad you gals are going." He cupped his hands around April's ample waist and lifted her into the wagon quite easily. Pax hovered by Laurel. He gave her a brotherly glare. "You can still stay home. Last chance, Sis."

"I'm going." She had no difficulty proclaiming that with great assurance. For the next six weeks, she'd have brand new vistas to sketch and paint.

His frown darkened. "I'm not bringing you back partway through the trip if you change your mind."

"There's no danger of that," she reassured him.

"Only," Caleb muttered, "because she's already out of her mind to go."

* * *

"Squatters are going to ruin the whole valley," Captain Wood growled as his men tore down yet another sign inviting tourists to stay at a tent-style hotel and eat at the restaurant.

"If it's not the businesses, it's the sheep," Gabe agreed.

"Sheep." One of the cavalrymen swore. "Stupid animals are grazing all the plant life clear down to the roots. Nothing left for the bighorn."

"Well, we ate mighty good mutton last night," another said.

Gabe shrugged. The squatters had received written and verbal notification to remove the sheep. The national preserve was for indigenous flora and fauna; not for flocks of sheep that grazed by cropping the grasses so close to the ground that the plants couldn't renew themselves, destroying the valleys. The cavalry didn't poach on the natural four-legged creatures for food, but sheep had been declared fair game. Since provender never rated as adequate, mutton became part of the menu. Gabe had to agree; the mutton came as a welcome change from the jerked beef he'd been eating for the past several weeks.

As a matter of fact, he'd ridden into Wawona to buy

supplies. The proprietor of the store and log hotel there charged relatively reasonable prices, so the cavalry tolerated his business.

Captain Wood ordered his troops, "Pay a visit to that encampment. Confiscate weapons."

"Yes, sir."

Gabe said nothing as the horsemen rode off. Their job demanded much and paid little, but each of them showed admirable diligence. They'd been like children when their cook discovered gumdrops in Gabe's supplies. He resolved to pick up more in Wawona.

"Where are you headed?" Captain Wood inquired.

"Wawona. Supplies. From there, Half Dome."

"Got enough ammunition?"

Gabe crooked a brow. "Same as always. Have yet to spend a single bullet."

The captain grinned. "That's why I allow you to keep arms."

"I'm grateful." With that, Gabe rode off, his packhorse obediently trotting in his wake.

The closer he drew to Wawona, the more tourists Gabe spotted. Some were here to enjoy the beauty, but most irritated him. Groups of men came in hopes of proving to one another who was more masculine by trying daring feats on the rock faces of the majestic formations. More than a few had fallen, but still the challenge drew those with nothing better to do than prove their boasts. The cavalry had to confiscate firearms because those same men couldn't get it through their thick skulls that the animals within the confines of the preserve were to be left alone. Sighting a deer, bighorn, or bear, men automatically grabbed for a rifle. Left to their own devices, those men would hunt the fauna to extinction in just a few years.

His irritation turned to disgust when he rounded a bend and spied a group of wagons. Seated by the man driving the lead wagon was a dark-haired beauty dressed in more frills than most Boston debutantes. Above her head, she held a lacy shade parasol to protect her porcelain complexion. A lady like her had absolutely no business out here. Oh, she'd fit in perfectly with his mother's crowd. He could envision her embroidering pillow slips for the unfortunates while ensconced in a comfortable chair near the fireplace in a well-appointed parlor.

The other three wagons, well, they just reinforced Gabe's opinion. Three women dressed in simple calico, a dozen strapping young men, enough supplies to last the entire U.S. Cavalry for a season—she'd brought all of the comforts of home, including servants, to assure her ease during this grand adventure.

Why did people like her bother to come here at all? Yosemite's beauty was wild; a tame miss like her wouldn't dare soil her kid slippers by hiking up a path. She'd quake in those same slippers at the mere thought of standing on the precipice of one of the cliffs. And the idea of wind blowing through that oh-so-perfect coiffure? Never. She might as well send one of her servants into the store, have him buy some of the stereopticon pictures of the park, and head back home. She could technically say she'd been to Yosemite—even if she hadn't actually seen a bit of it.

Irritated with himself for wasting thoughts on a woman, Gabe kneed his mount toward the store. He swung out of the saddle, hitched the mare, and gave her an appreciative pat before going inside.

"Rutlidge." The proprietor greeted him with a curt nod.

Gabe looked about. "Business is booming, I see."

"Had several big parties come through in the past week. I'm expecting fresh stock in a few days or so."

Neither piece of news pleased Gabe. He wandered about, trying to piece together supplies from what little remained while resolving to create a few caches of supplies the next time he got his hands on decent provisions.

Half a dozen cans of smoked oysters, a gallon-sized rectangular tin of hard tack, five pounds of cornmeal, and matches. He thumped his basket on the counter. "Any gum drops?"

"Nope."

"Lemon drops or peppermints?"

"Nope. Cleaned out. I did get in a nifty new candy. Looky here." The storekeeper pulled a box from beneath the counter and opened it. Lifting out a black shape, he boasted, "Licorice. See?" He held it to his lips. "Shaped like a pipe, no less. I'm betting little boys'll pester their parents to buy 'em. They'll sell like hotcakes."

"No doubt." Gabe thought about the cavalrymen. "I'll take three dozen."

"That's the whole box!"

"Then I proved your point—they'll sell like hotcakes. On the other hand, I don't know why you'd sell something like this to children. Smoking might well be fashionable for men, but I've always considered it a filthy habit. Children don't need to be encouraged toward such vices."

"There's nothing wrong with boys wanting to be like their fathers."

"Agreed." Gabe gave him a bored look. "But fathers need to be good examples."

"And you have children?" The proprietor's voice took on an edge.

"Not a one," Gabe admitted in a pleased tone. "I'm not the type to be tied down." He paid for his order, left the store, and proceeded to pack the odd collection onto his spare horse.

Once done, Gabe looked up just in time to see the princess sweep into the Wawona Hotel.

The sight didn't surprise him in the least.

three

"Oh, this is marvelous!" Laurel stretched out on the big iron bedstead. The featherbed billowed around her, then settled enough for her to turn and study the beautiful view out her window.

"Enjoy it while you can." April bounced on the other side of the bed. "Tomorrow we'll be roughing it."

Kate stood over at the window. "Come here, Johnna. Look at this."

Johnna limped across the plank floor. "I got me a blister bigger'n Noah's ark. Any of you bring 'long doctorin' things?"

April laughed. "Are you kidding? Mama Lovejoy put together a box from her herbal room, and Polly and her husband made a whole medical kit. Polly said it's the Dr. Eric Walcott nothing-you-can't-treat crate."

"Now jest you all hold yore horses." Johnna held up a hand. "Ain't puttin' one of them plasters on my blister. I heared they make a body itch sommat fierce."

"Not," Laurel announced, "when you use the special talcum powder that goes along with them." She got off the bed. "Kate, come with me. We'll go to the wagon and get what we need. April, you and Johnna freshen up. We girls are going to have tea this afternoon down in that restaurant. I aim to have us enjoy all the luxuries available before we head deep into this wilderness."

Johnna whirled around. "We're gonna eat in the restaurant? For true?"

"Absolutely." Laurel bobbed her head. "Mama slipped me some extra money for us girls to enjoy ourselves."

Kate giggled. "Mama gave me some money, too."

April twined her arm with Johnna. "Now how do you like that? Laurel's mother is a famous artist, and Kate's mother is an heiress. The two of us are just poor tag-along relations who will have to pity one another."

"Pity's gonna taste right fine at a restaurant tea table," Johnna declared. "I ain't niver gone to a fancy tea afore. S'pose I oughtta fix up my hair, even iff'n it'll all be 'neath my hat."

Laurel swept her shawl about her shoulders. "April will help you with your hair. I've taught her all my tricks, and she's great at making hair look quite fetching. Before she does, though, we're going to get one thing straight: There's never any pity at our table. We always share."

"We most certainly do," Kate agreed. She smoothed up her stocking and tugged her skirts back into order. "So after we have tea, we're going to shop at the store."

"My treat," Laurel inserted.

Kate obligingly nodded and kept right on talking so the others couldn't protest. "I heard they don't have much in the way of food left in the store, but who cares?"

"I packed enough food to feed a shipload of passengers for a month," April declared.

"Exactly. So we're going to look at the other things the proprietor has." Kate spread her hands wide. "What's a trip without a souvenir?"

"What's a sou-veneer?" Johnna wondered.

"A keepsake," April told her. "Something special you take home from a trip or a visit to remind you of the grand time you had."

"A heartful of memories'll do me jest fine," Johnna stated. "I don't need some expensive doodad to remind me of where I've been."

"But think about your brothers and sisters and cousins back home." Kate reached for the doorknob. "You, Peter, and Ulysses are the only ones to come this year. It'll be a couple of years before anyone else from MacPherson Ranch visits Yosemite. Don't you think they'd all like to see a little something from this place?"

"You gotta point," Johnna allowed. "But then I'm gonna cook extry to make up fer it. I don't take no charity. None of the MacPhersons do."

Laurel whipped off her shawl. "You listen to me, Johnna MacPherson. We're family. Oh, I know—maybe not legally, by blood, but by heart we are. We share our family picnics, celebrate things together, and have wept in grief beside one another. After all of that, do you think money matters one whit?"

Johnna winced. "Guess not."

"Good. Then no more nonsense. None from you, either, April Chance. In fact. . ." She grabbed her reticule. "You're each going to have your share of money to spend as you wish so we don't have to go through this absurd conversation again."

"You mean I'll be paying cash money at the restaurant, all by myself?" Johnna gaped at Laurel.

Laurel paused a moment. "No. After all, it was my idea, and I've invited you to be my guest. You'll be shopping in the store." She peeled out two five-dollar bills and gave one to April and the other to Johnna. "No being practical. Mama specified that we were supposed to fritter this money away because vacations are for fun."

"Fritter away five whole dollars?" Johnna looked at April, then back at the bill in her hand. "I ain't niver had one dollar all my own. I cain't 'magine what to do with five!"

"Mama was a gambler's daughter," Laurel reminded Johnna. "She knows what it's like to wish for something and not get it. That's why she wanted us to all have some cash to spend. Money isn't any good if all you do is hoard it. If we go home and haven't spent it, she'll be hurt."

"But five whole dollars," Johnna half squeaked.

"Mama painted a picture specially, just to make the money for us girls to spend. You know how much fun she has painting. It'll make her so happy to know someone's enjoying her art while we're enjoying ourselves."

"Well"—April tugged the pins out of Johnna's hair—"we'll have to hurry to fix ourselves up for tea. Afterward, we'll shop extravagantly to make Aunt Delilah delirious."

"If this ain't the backwardest way of thinkin', I don't ken what is." Johnna flopped down into a chair.

Laurel and Kate slipped out the door, down the hall, and out to the wagon. Kate giggled. "Oh, you did a great job back there."

"You were a wonderful help. I was serious—we're family, and we've always shared. I'd love to see April and Johnna fritter away the money on silly things, but they won't. I bet they fret over every last cent."

"We won't let them." Kate grinned. "Even if they do that today, it's my turn to give them money on the way home. Their pride sure gets in the way of fun, doesn't it?"

"Not today." Laurel winked. "Now let's find that talc and Johnson & Johnson plasters. I hope they have stockings and shoes in the store. Johnna's blister is because she's wearing boots that are too big."

"Oh—is that why she's clomping like a two-ton mule?"

Laurel covered her mouth to keep from laughing. "Oh, Kate! Only you would say it that way."

"It's the truth."

❧

"It's the truth," the storekeeper told Gabe. "I checked the back room. You're welcome to go back and see for yourself."

Gabe groaned. He'd forgotten salt. Of all the necessities, how could he have forgotten that? He'd turned his horses around and come back, only to discover the store was out of it. A man could do without a lot of things, but salt rated as an absolute necessity.

"Restaurant might spare you a bit," a red-haired gal said from across the store. She gave him a guileless smile.

Gabe nodded. "Obliged for the thought, miss." The gal seemed downright pleasant. She'd been practical as could be, trying on sensible boots. Although he wasn't supposed to notice such things, Gabe also spied the stockings she'd draped over the arm of the chair. A man couldn't fault a woman for seeing to such basic necessities.

Then he compared her to the "princess" he'd seen earlier. She stood a row over, looking at a bunch of idiotic little gewgaws that held no value whatsoever. "Excuse me," she called to the proprietor. "Do you have more of these? I'd like. . .two, no three dozen. They're darling, don't you think, Kate?"

"Huh? Oh, yes. Darling."

"And don't you think Mama will love this cedar wood box?" The princess held up a box far too dinky to hold anything reasonable. "The fragrance is enchanting. It reminds me of the Bible verses about the great temple."

Gabe turned to Mr. Hutchings. "Well, I'm thinking of Lot's wife. All I want is a pillar of salt. Guess I'll head toward the restaurant."

"We just dined there," the princess said. "The food was fabulous."

"I don't know." The young woman next to her shook her head. "April's strudel back home is better, if you ask me."

Gabe headed out as the women continued to chatter about all of the fancy food their cook back home made. He wanted to be away from these tourists. Yes, he reminded himself, the preserve was for everyone to enjoy—especially those who lived in the city and couldn't appreciate nature on a daily basis. But some of these people—they simply didn't get it. They came to nature and dragged the worst parts of civilization along. They represented everything he'd come here to escape.

⁂

Mmm-mmm-mmm. The early morning breeze carried the aroma of food—real food. Woman-cooked, mouth-watering, heap-your-plate-full, my-mouth-died-and-went-to-heaven fixings. Gabe closed his eyes and told himself he didn't need it. Didn't want it. Then called himself a liar.

He'd come back late last night and made do with jerked beef, even though he smelled the tempting fragrance of stew. The noise of several young men and the higher, softer voices of women kept him away. If it weren't so dark, he would have packed up and skulked off. He wanted nothing to do with rowdy campers. Tossing off the thick wool blanket he used as a bedroll, Gabe told himself to ignore the smell of bacon. Except his nose forgot to obey, and he sniffed again.

That did it. He wasn't going to stick around here another day. This amounted to torture. Stomping off toward the stream, he tried to decide where he ought to go to avoid the crowds of tourists. Peace, quiet, and a lack of tempting food smells—that wasn't asking so much, was it? He tossed his towel around his neck and twisted the ends in frustration. Once done with washing up, he'd dismantle his simple camp and—

He pulled to a dead halt.

four

Sitting on his rock by his stream, a dainty woman in pale pink ruffles with a parasol over her shoulder hummed in a lilting alto.

"What're you doing here?" Gabe demanded.

"Oh!" She twisted about and dropped whatever she'd been holding. The parasol tumbled behind her, revealing abundant black hair all twisted up into some fancy arrangement. Her golden eyes stayed wide with fright as she stared at him.

He tamped back a groan. *The princess! In the back wilderness? I don't believe it.*

She blinked and found her voice. "I'm camping. What are you doing here?"

It didn't escape Gabe's notice that she'd raised her volume a slight bit with each word so the last one came out at respectable volume. Clever little minx hadn't shouted for help, but she'd made certain whomever she was with would hear her. He didn't respond to her question. Instead, he waited in silence for her rescuer.

"Laurel!" Two young men dashed around a stand of trees and skidded to a halt beside her. The taller studied Gabe with no small measure of ire. "Breakfast is ready, Sis. You go on back. You," he ordered, nodding toward Gabe, "leave her be."

"Don't be rude, Pax." The young woman stooped to pick up a sketch pad and charcoal sketch pencil. "Invite the gentleman to join us at the table since you made mention of breakfast."

"Wouldn't do any harm, I suppose," the other young man said.

Pax shifted his weight and moved his right hand in such a

way that Gabe could clearly see he wore a sidearm. "We don't want any trouble. You're welcome to eat, but afterward, you leave our gals alone."

Gabe rested his hands on his hips and tilted his head back as he let out a bellow of a laugh. "Believe me, women are a complication I don't want in my life."

"We didn't, either," the shorter man muttered. "But we brought 'em along for cooking and so we could keep arms."

"Well, thank you so much for your complimentary opinions of our companionship," the woman simpered. She turned in a swirl of ruffles and headed away.

"Betcha we pay for that tonight, Ulysses," the one named Pax said with a crooked grin. "Laurel's supposed to make supper."

"What can she do to fish?" Ulysses folded his arms across his broad chest. "I think we're safe."

"You'll go hungry if you plan to fish here," Gabe informed them. "Nothing bites for a good ways up or downstream from this spot."

"You know a good fishin' spot?" Ulysses perked up.

"He can tell us about it over breakfast. If we don't get there, everything'll be gone." Pax tilted his head toward their camp.

Gabe felt torn for a second. He could refuse, go on his way, and be free—or he could eat some of that tempting food, be minimally sociable for half an hour, and then decamp. His stomach growled. "Give me a second."

Ulysses gave him a baffled look.

Having grown up in high society ingrained certain expectations. Gabe shed most of them while alone in the wilderness, but he'd be in the company of ladies. Decency demanded he not appear at their table in his current state. Dipping the end of his towel into the cold stream, he muttered, "I'm wearing half the park."

Pax chortled. "The rest of us are wearing the other half."

By the time they made it to the camp, Gabe had swiped himself fairly clean and combed his wild hair. In retrospect, it amazed him Miss Laurel hadn't taken one look at him and screamed herself hoarse.

Comprised of four wagons and two tents, the campsite looked surprisingly simple—even minimalistic. Surprised at the lack of so-called civilized trappings, Gabe looked around. "Is this everything you brought?"

Ulysses pointed up to several bundles hanging by ropes from high tree limbs. "We've hung the vittles. Bears won't get into it thataway."

"The girls are sleeping in a tent," Pax scoffed.

"Are you going to introduce us to our guest?" a redheaded girl called over to them. Gabe recognized her as the one who'd been trying on boots at the store in Wawona.

"Gabe Rutledge." Gabe looked at the heavily laden breakfast table and felt his mouth water. "Thank you for inviting me to your meal."

"Grab a plate and have a seat," Pax said. Most of the men already sat around on the ground in clumps with heaps of flapjacks and several rashers of bacon on graniteware plates.

"We already asked a blessing," someone stated.

Pax thumped his chest. "You've gathered I'm Pax. Paxton Chance. That there's Ulysses MacPherson. Peter MacPherson's to your left. He's Ulysses's cousin. Any other P name, that'll be one of my brothers. The T's are all brothers, and so are the C's. I won't bother you with callin' them out. The food'll go cold, and no sane man would remember ten names all at once."

"Obliged." Gabe found himself liking this crew. They bedrolled under the stars, sat on the ground instead of hauling up all sorts of furniture, and showed a practicality sadly lacking in most other groups who came to camp out. He nodded toward the small knot of women. "Breakfast smells wonderful. Thank you."

"You're welcome." Three voices blended like a small chorus in unison. The fourth, Miss Laurel's, waited a beat. "I cannot take any credit for my cousins' cooking, but you're still welcome."

"Laurel uses the early morning light to draw. She makes up for it by cooking supper most often," Pax said as he shoved a plate at Gabe.

Gabe accepted the plate and followed Ulysses down the table. Ulysses forked no less than a half-dozen flapjacks onto his plate, drowned them with syrup, and piled several rashers of bacon atop the meal. Gabe took three of the huge flapjacks, but by the time he lifted the jug of syrup, Pax had dumped two more on his plate.

"No use goin' hungry. We have plenty."

Sitting on the ground with the men, Gabe wolfed down his meal. Every bite tasted as delicious as the first.

"What're you doing here?" someone asked him.

"Exploring. Appreciating."

"Your accent is eastern. Not New York. Boston? Chicago?" Ulysses asked.

Gabe nodded. He didn't want to be specific. Most folks on this coast didn't know of the Boston Rutlidges, but those who did immediately treated him differently. Greed shone in their eyes, and Gabe didn't want money to be an issue when he dealt with others. Part of traveling away from Boston was to know no one pursued him for his money. He'd learned that bitter lesson a million times, but Arabella's scheme was the final straw. And to think he'd been ready to propose to her!

Well, I don't need a woman. I don't need anybody. Sure, he thought as he swallowed the last bite of bacon, *food's much better and companionship is good, but I'm doing fine without those a good portion of the time. I'm better off on my own.*

Then again, watching the brothers and cousins teasing one another hit a soft spot. Gabe missed Stanford. His younger brother viewed their privileged world with a great deal of humor and managed to get along swimmingly. He'd been the voice of sanity on several occasions, and to his credit, when things went wrong with Arabella, Stanford wholeheartedly supported Gabe's decision to get away. Gabe held no doubts whatsoever that Stanford was running the business without a single hitch and actually enjoyed the daily grind. He'd been born and bred to do just that—and Gabe, though capable, never once enjoyed any of it.

A nominal believer in something nebulous called Fate, Gabe figured Stanford was where he belonged—in control of the family fortune. Then, too, Gabe knew he'd landed just where he belonged—free of such encumbrances and alone where he could live without the burdens of society and appreciate nature.

Gabe wondered about this Chance family. Someone said they'd asked a blessing on the food. That meant at least some of them probably trusted in God. Having grown up in a home where grace was said and everyone attended church, Gabe didn't exactly disbelieve; he just wasn't sure he really did believe. How many of the young people around him still questioned all they'd been told?

His musings left Gabe unsettled. A void opened inside him. *It's just that I'm missing Stanford—that's all.*

"So you were gonna tell us about a good fishin' spot," Ulysses poked at him with a fork.

"Fishin'? Nah. I wanna climb that monstrous rock." Someone else pointed straight ahead.

"Half Dome," Gabe provided the name of the formation. "It's a healthy climb. Great view."

"You've been up there?" Laurel asked. She set down her half-full plate and gave him an enthused look. Intelligence glittered in her golden eyes. "What is the view like? How far can you see, and what details stay in focus?"

"She sounds more like a camera than a girl," Paxton muttered.

Gabe ignored that comment and answered, "The view is stupendous. Close up, massive formations of granite lie all around you. As you look down and out, the stream looks like a silvery blue thread. Trees are blended splotches of green. People are tiny specks, if you see them at all."

"What're we waiting for?" someone across from him said. "Let's go!"

The reaction felt like an interruption. Always deeply moved by the views from the elevated vistas in Yosemite, Gabe enjoyed sharing his observations. He could have gone on to explain so much more, include the interesting details he'd seen. From the eager way Miss Laurel leaned forward, she wanted to hear more, but it wasn't to be. These young men would see it for themselves, and in their zeal, they'd not considered the women wouldn't have that opportunity.

"Best ask what we need to take, Packard," Paxton said.

Packard. He's P, so he's Paxton's brother. Paxton called Laurel Sis. Gabe forgave them their youthful impetuousness and tried to put the pieces together.

"Well, what do you recommend, Gabe?" Packard leaned forward.

Gabe didn't tell the young man his shirt was sopping up syrup from his plate. No use embarrassing the kid. "It's too late to go up today. In fact, we're too far away. Distances are deceiving here. You need to have everything gathered and at the base first thing in the morning. Someone built a wooden ladder to get you to the first level, but from there, you'll require rope—lots of it."

"How much?"

"I recommend fifty yards per man. You're all wearing sensible clothing and boots, so that's good. You'll each need a hat to keep away the glare, and you should take water and nutritious, easy-to-carry food."

"I'll have the food all packed," one of the gals promised.

"You're not going. None of you girls is." One of the black-haired men rose and dumped his plate into a bucket of suds.

"Who's staying behind with them?" another asked.

"Not me," the men all proclaimed at once, then looked around at each other.

"This is why we didn't want girls along," someone said from behind Gabe.

"Tanner Chance, you just said you were glad we came along when you heaped all that food on your plate," a young blond in a blue calico dress insisted.

"How long will you be here?" Gabe asked.

"Six weeks." A redhead with a rowdy-looking beard shook Gabe's hand. "I'm Peter MacPherson. I reckon that's plenty of time. We men can break into teams. One'll explore whilst the other fishes and guards the women."

Gabe nodded.

"You think I'm going to spend half of my trip babysitting the girls?" One of the men smacked his hat against his thigh in disgust.

"What makes you think we want to sit at the campground all the time?" Laurel asked.

"Yeah. We want to go on hikes," said the blond. She flashed Gabe a smile. "And I'm Kate. This is April, and Johnna's standing by Laurel."

"Miss." Gabe nodded in a mannerly fashion as he made a mental note that each had different colored hair: Laurel was raven-haired, Kate was the blond, April had brunette hair, and Johnna unmistakably belonged to the red-haired MacPhersons. "There are pleasant meadows you ladies could walk through."

"I want to climb up to a waterfall and stand in the spray," April confessed as she leaned across the table.

Gabe shook his head. "The waterfalls are at extreme elevations. You'll see them but not stand in one." Seeing the sparkle in her eyes dim, he added on, "Bridal Veil Falls flows into Bridal Veil Creek. You could wade in it. That's all west of here."

"I saw that on the map!" April perked up.

"Perhaps Mr. Rutlidge has some recommendations as to where we ought to go or what we should see," Laurel suggested. "He seems to know the preserve quite well."

"You don't mind, do you?" Paxton yanked a map from his pocket and started unfolding it without waiting for an answer. From the rumpled, much-folded appearance of that map, Gabe surmised the young man had studied it several times.

"Put it on the table so we can all gather 'round and see," Peter demanded.

In a few moments, the nearly empty platters on the table were divested of whatever food remained and tossed into the wash bucket. Paxton spread the map out on the table, and coffee mugs soon held the ends down.

Gabe glanced at the map. He'd seen several—most were poorly drawn. "You have a decent map. The distances on it look to be fairly accurate."

"Tobias and I looked at half a dozen before we settled on this one," Pax said as he poked his forefinger at a spot. "To my reckoning, we're about here."

"Yes. Half Dome is straight ahead. Bridal Veil Falls is here, and the creek flows. . ." Gabe trailed his finger along the path. "Fishing in it is only so-so. The fishing in the Merced River's better."

"Good to know," someone said.

Gabe scanned the intent faces around him. "Fishing is permitted, but this is a preserve. You only catch what you'll eat. No dragging fish out just for the sport of it."

Peter gave him an outraged look. "We ain't stupid. Who

kills jest for the sake of it? Then there won't be 'nuff fish for the next year."

"You'd be surprised," Gabe said. "Men come here for the adventure and lose all common sense. None of the streams down here have been supplemented. Three of the lakes northwest of here have additional trout, thanks to Mr. Kibbie."

"Are there plans for stocking the rivers?"

"No. The cavalry is here just for safety and preservation—they're spread mighty thin. No one's available to do it."

A flash of pale pink made Gabe turn. Laurel stood a foot away, holding a huge coffeepot. "Anyone want more coffee?"

Five mugs in heavily callused fists shot toward her. Not a single man said a word. Gabe waited until she filled them all, then extended his mug. "Thank you, I'd appreciate more."

She gave him a stunned look, then smiled. "You're welcome, Mr. Rutlidge."

"The girls wanted to go to Tuolumne Meadows."

"Forget it, Tanner," Paxton growled. "They can see meadows anywhere. We can't waste time on that."

Laurel's lashes dropped, and the corners of her mouth tightened.

Gabe cleared his throat. "Actually, the meadows are worth seeing. They spread out for miles, and wildlife abounds. Take a look at your map. If you start out at the meadows, then travel southwest from there, you'll hit the sites most visitors come for—Clouds Rest, Half Dome—"

"We already saw Sentinel Dome and Glacier Point on the way here," Tobias said.

"So what if we cross the creek and go to North Dome?" Enthusiasm colored Ulysses's voice.

"Hold on. Miss April wanted to see falls. I recommend you spend time seeing Vernal Falls and Nevada Falls. They're on this side and basically on your way. Your map doesn't remark on them, but they're breathtaking. Then you can cross the creek and see North Dome."

"From there," Caleb decided, "we'll hit Yosemite Falls. See, Sis? I'm making sure you'll get your fill of falls. And then us guys'll climb El Capitan. We can cross back over the river someplace."

"Go farther west," Gabe advised, "then double back so you see Bridal Veil Falls. You can trace it through the creek on your way back out."

"You all rushed me through them great big trees on the way in," Johnna said from the washtub. "I want a day to wander 'round them on our way home."

"We got water and trees back home," one of the younger men scoffed. "The rocks are what make this place."

"We've got rocks back home, too—just nowhere near this size," Caleb said. "If we go by Gabe's plan, everyone ought to see something to please them."

"Now about that fishin'." Ulysses jabbed Gabe with his elbow and bent over the map. "How's about you showin' us where a feller cain hope to land him a big old trout?"

Gabe stood in the huddle of men and pored over the map. They asked question after question, and he patiently answered them as he started to pair faces and names.

A platter of sandwiches landed on the table. Gabe's head shot up. He gave Laurel a startled look. "I lost track of time."

She nodded. "I think the time's well spent. You're probably saving us days of backtracking by helping our men figure out where to go."

"Eat up." Calvin shoved a sandwich into Gabe's hand.

Gabe chuckled. He'd never had anyone offer him a meal in such a straightforward way. Back home, there would have been a formal invitation, a well-set table, and servants. Even when his family dined casually, they passed platters. When he ate with the cavalrymen, the cook slopped food onto the plates. Something about the simple slapping of a sandwich into his hand, of skipping plates and diving in appealed to Gabe. "Thanks."

"If you're just ambling along, you're welcome to join us," Paxton said.

Gabe swallowed his bite. The food tempted him. The male companionship appealed to him. But he didn't want women around any more than these men did. Especially not Princess Laurel, who listened to him so intently. The woman was far too easy on the eye, and Gabe refused to stumble into that pitfall again. He shrugged. "The offer's nice, but I prefer to be on my own."

&

Laurel didn't realize she'd been holding her breath until Gabe turned down the invitation. Then she couldn't decide whether to be glad or disappointed by his refusal.

He'd startled her this morning. She'd been so intent on her sketch that his voice scared her. Luckily, she'd dropped her charcoal pencil instead of making an unsightly streak across her piece. It would have been a shame. She wanted to finish that drawing, add a touch of pastel color to it, and give it to Daddy as a gift.

But Mr. Rutlidge. He scared her in a thrilling way. Oh, men back home thronged around her. She knew they all wanted a pretty woman to squire about. Mama and Daddy never minced words—they told her she was lovely to look at, but beauty was fleeting and proved no accomplishment. God created her as one of His works of art, but it was her responsibility to do all she could to become beautiful on the inside. Any man who wanted her only as a decoration probably wouldn't look for, let alone appreciate, the inward beauty her parents urged her to cultivate. She'd been interested in a few young men from neighboring spreads in a fleeting fashion, but when they treated her like a stupid, helpless woman, her interest waned.

Only Mr. Rutlidge didn't fawn after her; he almost ignored her! He'd sounded outraged that she'd been by the creek. He didn't want her around. In fact, he'd made his opinion of women being a bother quite clear. Then why had he been so polite to the girls? Why had he made a point of including their desires while helping the boys plot out their plan? The man qualified as a bundle of contradictions.

Laurel bit into her sandwich and tried to make sense of it, but she couldn't.

"That there's one fine buck," Johnna whispered.

Brows lifted, Laurel asked, "Which one?"

April tossed an apple into Laurel's lap and giggled. "Ours are all good, but only one of those men over at the table is. . . dreamy."

"Oh, no, April." Laurel shook her forefinger at her cousin. "You did this same thing when Eric arrived in Reliable Township. You mooned over him, and all we heard was 'Dr. Walcott this' and 'Dr. Walcott that.' I'm saying here and now, you're not going to make a ninny of yourself just because a handsome man stumbled into our camp."

"So you think he's handsome, do you?" Kate gave Laurel a triumphant look.

"The real beauty of a person is on the inside. We know nothing about him," Laurel said primly, then quickly took another bite so she wouldn't be expected to say anything more.

"I cain tell plenty about him." Johnna settled into a more comfortable spot on the grass. "He talks like a man who's had plenty of book learning. His manners are re-fined. Niver heared a man say thankee as much as he's done."

"He's a good listener. Attentive," April tacked on.

"But he's just wandering around Yosemite—and for a good long while. What kind of man doesn't have a job?" Kate polished her apple on her sleeve.

"None of this matters one whit," Laurel announced. "He's going his way, and we're going ours."

"More's the pity," April sighed.

Laurel shot her a behave-yourself look, then glanced at Johnna. Johnna had a sound head on her shoulders. She could be counted on to say something to bring April to her senses.

Johnna smiled at Laurel. Laurel felt a burst of relief.

"April, ain't nuthin' wrong with settin' yore heart on a buck. Jest be sure he's not all antlers and no muscle."

April's face scrunched up in confusion. "What is that supposed to mean?"

Laurel resisted the urge to bob her head. *I wondered the same thing.*

"Well, he might be real showy, but that don't get no work done." Johnna bobbed her head as if to put exclamation marks after her sage comment.

Laurel wasn't quite sure exactly how much wisdom was behind those words, but she shifted her sandwich to her other hand and patted April. "She's right. We've had plenty of saddle tramps come through Chance Ranch. Some of the best workers have been the homeliest or the scrawniest. You can't make snap judgments."

"I'm not going to have an opportunity to find out, either," April pouted. "He's not going to join us."

"Well, if you ask me, it's just as well," Kate declared. "A man who wears expensive gear like that and doesn't have a job gives me the willies."

He gives me the willies, too—but for entirely different reasons, Laurel thought.

five

"One last thing before I go." Gabe looked at the men still milling about him. "Tell your women to stop wearing perfume."

"Hadn't noticed that they did." Paxton scratched his side.

"They do. All of them." *Especially Laurel.* He'd not been around women for months, and the slightest hint of cologne struck him full force. The other three women wore fragrances that were light and pleasant; Laurel favored something outrageously feminine that left a tempting sweetness in its wake something akin to a luscious, ripe berry. "Wasps and bees are more likely to sting a woman if she's wearing a scent."

"They packed half the world to come on the trip," Tanner groused. "We shouldn't be surprised they brought perfume."

"Tell them to leave it in the bottle." Gabe pretended not to notice how abrupt he sounded. "It's for their own good."

"Rather you told 'em," Tobias said. "My sister's far more likely to listen to you than to me."

A rumble of agreements filled the air.

Gabe crooked his brow in disbelief.

"You don't have a sister, do you?" Paxton asked.

"No."

"They have a habit of digging in their heels at the dumbest times," Paxton explained. "Our folks drilled manners into those girls. They'll listen to you far better than they will to us. It's for their own good."

Gabe let out a bark of a laugh and shouldered his way through the men. He walked past a string of some of the finest horseflesh he'd ever seen and paused. "Nice horses."

"Chance horses. Family business." Caleb's chest swelled. "Any time you need a mount, we're the ones to see."

"If these are any sample, I'd agree." Gabe strode on over to the knot of women. They'd cleaned up the lunch gear and were huddled around something. "Ladies."

They all straightened up. Laurel slammed her sketchbook shut. "Hello."

Gabe wanted to know what she'd been drawing, but it would be rude to ask. What was it about this woman that drove him nuts? He wanted to grab her book and flip through it, to have her tell him about what she'd sketched and why. He felt absurd just standing there, so he cleared his throat and resorted to the social conventions that never failed to rescue a man from uncomfortable situations. "I wanted to thank you again for the meals. They were quite tasty."

"You're welcome." April grinned at him.

His gaze swept over them all, then settled back on Laurel. "One other thing. Bees and wasps abound here. They're attracted to scent. Your perfumes are quite appealing, but I'm afraid the only things you'll attract are stings. I suggest you forego wearing those scents while you're in Yosemite."

"It's not perfume," Laurel informed him in her melodious voice. "Polly, our cousin, specially makes each of us our own shampoo and soap."

"Use it, and suffer the consequences."

The other girls nodded. Laurel paled. Her reaction disappointed Gabe. Were the little luxuries so essential to her? *Just like Arabella, the trappings were all-important to her.* He'd pegged Miss Laurel Chance correctly. She acted like a little princess.

"Have an enjoyable stay in Yosemite." He turned and left. The walk back to his own site took no time at all. In a matter of minutes, Gabe rolled up his wool blanket, secured it behind the saddle, and broke camp.

Just as he swung up into his saddle, Paxton rode over. He tossed a bundle into Gabe's lap. "The girls thought you might want supper since you're traveling today."

Whatever rested inside the bundle smelled outstanding. Gabe couldn't imagine that strangers treated him with such hospitality—especially since he'd been so rude to Laurel this morning. "One whiff of this, and I'm ready to eat it now."

Pax chuckled. "They were right—you've been without decent cooking for a while. You know where we're going and about how long we'll be at each spot. You're always welcome to join up with us. Meals are included."

"It's tempting, but I'll pass it up."

"God go with you." Paxton reached over to shake hands.

"How about if He stays with you."

~

"It's not safe for you to be off on your own like this."

Laurel wheeled around. "Mr. Rutlidge!" He'd ridden away over more than two weeks ago, and she'd resigned herself to the fact that they'd never meet again. "What a pleasant surprise. I heard you coming, but I thought it was one of the men. They're around the bend, swimming and fishing."

His eyes widened and his lips parted in surprise as he stepped closer and studied the watercolor.

Laurel shuffled to the side so he could see the rest of the painting she'd been doing. She hadn't allowed herself much space, but this was the vantage point she wanted. The easel barely fit between her and the tree.

The moment she saw this spot, Laurel had known she had to paint it. Sunlight filtered through a variety of trees, setting a thousand hues of green alight, then glittered on the ripples of the stream. A solitary tree had fallen across the stream at its narrowest point. Roots long since gone, that tree formed a bridge of sorts that promised adventures to places unseen.

After a short while, Gabe's silence unnerved her. Laurel reached out to fuss with a brush, but his big hand manacled her wrist. "Don't touch it."

"Why not?"

"Because it's perfect just as it is. I want it. How much?"

Laurel looked from his suntanned face to the painting. "Thank you for the compliment, but it's not for sale."

"Everything has a price." His hold on her wrist loosened. "It's a wonderful piece, Laurel."

Laurel twisted free of his hold. "My mother is a professional artist. I just dabble. I—"

"Dabble? Woman, this is awe-inspiring. You captured the very essence of this spot."

"It's kind of you to say so, but I already have plans for this. It's for my Aunt Lovejoy."

"Paint her another."

"It doesn't work that way." Laurel gave him an exasperated look. "I could copy this, but it wouldn't be an exact duplicate. The shades and shadows will be different because my lighting will change. I'd be happy to paint you something else if you'd like."

"I'm willing to pay top dollar for this one."

Laurel frowned. "It's not for sale. Contrary to your assertion, everything doesn't have a price."

Gabe folded his arms across his chest. "Then what else do you have? I want to see what you've been painting and drawing—everything you've done since you arrived."

"Everything?" She gave him a shocked look. The man didn't understand how she either had a needle, a pencil, or a paintbrush in her hand all of her waking hours.

The breeze lifted the edge of her painting. He gently smoothed the corner back down and moved to serve as a windbreak. "Is this dry now?"

"Watercolors dry almost instantly."

"Good. I'll carry your easel." He started to bend forward to collapse the legs.

Laurel planned to stay here for some time yet. She'd brought all she needed to paint a few pictures. Then again, Gabe Rutlidge didn't exactly leave room for dissent. The man knew what he wanted and plowed toward it with a single-mindedness she'd not seen in any of the men who came courting.

Not that he's courting me, she quickly reminded herself.

"I don't think you know what you're asking. I've been quite busy with my artwork since we've arrived."

"Then I'm in for a pleasant surprise."

"You flatter me."

He lifted the easel. "Miss Chance, if even one of your other pieces comes close to the beauty of this watercolor, I'll be a happy man."

"Then let's see if you can find something that'll please you." She walked along beside him carrying her brushes in a jar as well as her paint box. "My brothers and cousins have enjoyed your advice regarding rock climbing."

"Good. Did you have a good time at Tuolumne Meadows?"

"Oh, the meadows are magnificent! I could have stayed there forever." She paused a moment as he cupped her elbow to help her over a branch that lay in their path, then murmured, "Thank you. And thank you, too, for talking the boys into going to the meadows. Left to their own devices, we'd probably camp in the shadow of the gigantic rocks and never move!"

"There are always bigger, more interesting rocks. Their collective sense of adventure would drive them to move on." He gave her a boyish grin. "I know whereof I speak."

"How long have you been wandering through Yosemite?"

"Since early spring."

Laurel shook her head. "I can't imagine how lonely that

must be. I love my family. It's huge, and I'm always surrounded by noise. There are times when I wish I could have a little time alone, some peace and quiet—but more than a day or two, and I'd be forlorn."

"How many children are in your family?"

"Do you mean, how many children do my parents have, or how many children are on the ranch?"

"You all live together?" He halted and gave her a startled look.

"Daddy and four of his brothers all live on the ranch—each has his own home. The older boys live together in a separate cabin, and we girls have a cabin of our own, too."

"The place must be massive."

"We have plenty of room." She didn't specify the acreage. It seemed boastful. Then again, when they'd gone to Reliable to settle, all six of the brothers and their mother had a right to claim land. Farsighted, they'd grabbed as much as they could and worked hard to improve it. The only one who had moved away was her uncle Logan, but enough land and work remained for all of them. God had blessed their efforts.

"So Paxton and Packard are your brothers. How many more do you have?"

"Three more." She laughed. "We girls have a cabin of our own because we're abysmally outnumbered. Altogether, there are fourteen boys and three of us girls living on Chance Ranch."

He whistled under his breath.

"How many children in your family, Mr. Rutlidge?"

"Just two. I have a younger brother." They arrived back at the campsite. "Where shall I set your easel?"

"Over by the tent, please." Laurel heard voices. "Johnna? April? Are you in the tent?"

"Yes." April stuck her head out of the flap. "We were—oh! Hello, Mr. Rutlidge! Johnna, guess who's here?"

"You just said his name, you silly goose." Johnna exited the tent. "Fancy seein' you again, Mr. Rutlidge. Did we catch up with you, or did you catch up with us?"

He chuckled. "I think we met in the middle."

"April and me—we were just deciding whether to take a hike or fix something special for supper. Kate's fishin' with the boys, and we'd have to drag someone away from his fishin' pole if we want to wander."

"After Laurel shows me her art, I'd be honored to escort you ladies on a walk."

"Oh, mercy." April laughed. "We won't have that walk for three days. Has she told you how much she's been doing?"

Gabe slanted a smile at Laurel. It made her heart skip a beat, then speed up. "I'm glad to hear it wasn't an exaggeration. The piece she did this morning is stupendous."

"Ain't fittin' for you to go in the tent. Me and April'll drag out the chest for you." Johnna nodded. "Laurel, the both of you go move the chairs to the shade. Sun's moved, and you'll burn worse'n a side of bacon on a griddle iff'n you sit in the bright of the day."

The girls ducked back into the tent, and Laurel busied herself by laying the paint box and brushes on the table. Being compared to a side of bacon somehow made her want to giggle, but she didn't dare. It would be rude.

Gabe leaned a little closer. "I could listen to that gal talk all day. She's as colorful as your painting." He waggled his brows. "It might not have seemed complimentary to you, but men happen to love the smell of bacon."

That did it. Laurel burst out laughing. Gabe's deep laughter mingled with hers as he moved the chairs into a patch of shade.

Laurel noticed he didn't just move two chairs—he moved all four so April and Johnna could join them. Gabe proved himself to be just as thoughtful the second they cleared the tent with her crate of art. He strode over, immediately hefted it away from them, and brought it to the shade. Standing in front of Laurel, he glanced down at the crate, then back at her. "I can see I'm in for a treat."

"The watercolors are in the two tablets on the right."

"And what's in the other tablets?" He set down the crate and surveyed the contents.

"Sketches. Pastels. Oils take too long to dry. I tried one, but it got bugs in it and smeared."

"The bugs were attracted to the scent you're wearing." He gave her a stern look.

Unwilling to tell him she'd broken out in a terrible rash from the lye soap, Laurel changed the subject. "Perhaps I'll make lunch while you leaf through—"

"No." He sat down and gently tugged her wrist to get her to sit beside him.

"Show him your meadows first," April urged.

"No, the one of the butterfly. 'Tis the one I favor most." Johnna settled in next to Laurel.

"I'll see them all." Gabe reached into the box and took out the first tablet. He handled it deftly, but with care. Opening the cover, he stated, "I've always admired folks who could draw. I don't have in it me."

A charcoal pencil sketch of Tuolumne was the first piece. A sea of grass and wildflowers waved across the page, swept by the breeze. Gabe didn't tear his gaze from it as he said in a low tone, "But you certainly have the talent, Miss Laurel. This is wondrous. I can see the blades bending in the wind. That's just how it looks, too."

"Thank you."

He soaked up that picture, then slowly turned to the next. . . and the next. "You captured the bark perfectly. I feel like I could touch this and pick up the rough texture. . . Mule deer step so daintily, don't they? You have her poised exactly the way they do—I don't know how you captured her in motion like that."

"I've always dabbled at home. Here, I can't seem to help myself. Something inside demands I sketch or paint. I can't explain it."

"Hit's a matter of the right seed in the right soil," Johnna declared. "You ken there's places in a garden what'll grow only a few thangs, but when those flower, they're fearsome fine. I 'spect same's true with you. You needed to come here to set your soul abloom."

Gabriel nodded. "Yosemite is like that for some of us. We come here, and it touches us deeply."

"I feel so close to God here," Laurel confessed.

Staring at the next sketch, Gabe murmured, "It shows."

He didn't flip through the books as she'd expected. Instead, he took time over each sketch—even the silly ones she'd done of her cousins and brothers. "Boots, huh?"

She laughed. "Look how scuffed up they are. Climbing is taking a terrible toll on their clothes—and we anticipated that, but I've never seen sorrier looking boots. By the time we make it back home, every last man is going to have to break in a new pair of boots."

"It's only shoe leather," April stated practically. "They've had such a good time, they won't mind a few blisters."

"Kate's mighty good with leather. She's been repairin' the boots regular-like."

"Is that so?" Gabe's chin lifted. "There's a rough spot on my packhorse's girth strap. I've been padding it with a scrap of cloth. Think she could fix it?"

"We'll ask her," Laurel said. "Leatherwork is where Kate's talent shines."

"It's plain to see where your talent lies," Gabe said as he looked at Laurel. He'd set aside a handful of sketches and a pair of watercolors. "We need to discuss these. I want to purchase them."

"I've never sold my work. You're welcome to take them."

"That's generous of you, but I insist on buying them. In fact, I'm hoping to buy a view of Bridal Veil Falls from you once you've been there. My mother would treasure that."

The thought that he wanted to buy something already had her off-balance. Laurel couldn't imagine he wanted to give her art as a gift. The thought stunned her. "I'm not sure what to think."

"Think about doing a watercolor of Bridal Veil," he shot back. "Do you have any pasteboard tubes so I can preserve these? I'd hate to have them get crumpled or dog-eared."

"No, I don't have anything like that."

"Jist use the back o' one of them pads of yourn," Johnna said. "That ought to work out."

"Good idea." Gabe rummaged through the box. "These two pads are the same size, and you've filled them both. If we take the back of this one but keep them stacked together, the pictures ought to be protected still. What do you say?"

"How do you intend to keep it curled shut?" Laurel wondered aloud.

"Twine. I carry some in my pack. It's handy stuff." Gabe went over to the packs he'd removed from his horses, rummaged for a few minutes, and then reappeared with a decent length of twine in his palm. "This will serve our needs."

"Yes, I think it'll work well." Laurel tore the back off of a pad.

Standing close, Gabe murmured, "Would you rather we spoke privately about the financial arrangements?"

"Honestly, I don't know what to do. I'm not a professional artist. Would a dollar be too much?"

"A dollar!"

six

Heat crept from Laurel's bosom to her face. She'd tried to estimate how much the paper, paint, and pastels cost, then add in a tiny bit for her time.

"Woman, that doesn't even begin to cover your costs, let alone remunerate you for your talent!"

Laurel could scarcely hear him for the relief that poured through her.

"I brought one of those Kodak cameras with me. I took all one hundred pictures and sent it back to Rochester. It was twenty-five dollars for the camera, and the developing and reloading of the film was another ten. The sad fact is, I'm no photographer. Scarcely a handful of the pictures turned out at all, and the lighting on them is such that I missed most of what I wanted to show."

"Let's do the arithmetic," April suggested. "You got one hundred photographs for thirty-five dollars. That comes to thirty-five cents per picture."

"No, it doesn't," Laurel protested as she rose. "It included film for one hundred more pictures."

"But not the developing," Gabe hastened to say. "Nor the shipping."

"So charge him thirty-five cents per picture," Johnna suggested. "That's fair, isn't it?"

"No, it's not." Gabe's voice rivaled a thunderclap. "I was attempting to illustrate that for thirty-five dollars, I didn't get a fraction of the value of these beautiful works of art."

Though rarely at a loss for words, Laurel stood in shocked silence. She'd seen others feel this way about Mama's pictures, but no one had ever been so moved over anything she'd done. The magnitude of knowing her art affected someone so profoundly washed over her.

Gabe folded his arms across his chest. "I want to commission a watercolor of Bridal Veil, but I can't if you and I don't come to a reasonable agreement regarding these other pieces. I refuse to cheat you simply because you're an undiscovered talent. Back in Boston or New York, I'd pay a pretty penny for anything like this—and believe me when I tell you it's of the same quality of the drawings and paintings shown in galleries back East."

"What do you think is reasonable?" Laurel half-croaked.

"Sixty dollars."

Her knees nearly buckled. Laurel blindly felt for the seat behind her and promptly folded herself back onto it before she fell. "Impossible!"

He shook his head. "You're a grand artist and a terrible businesswoman, Laurel Chance."

"Whilst she's thinkin' on that, d'you still have that camera?" Johnna grinned. "I've niver seen one. Oh—I seed the big ones them professional photographers cart around, but yourn sounds dreadful nice."

Thankful for the reprieve, Laurel watched as Gabe walked away and pulled the camera from his pack. He returned with not only the camera, but also a small stack of photographs. "These are the ones I kept—you can see they didn't turn out very well."

Laurel slowly shuffled through the pictures. "You're right. The lighting is wrong. These would have done better with early morning or late afternoon light so the shadows would give more depth and definition."

"So that's what it was. I figured I needed the noonday sun to make everything show up more clearly."

She smiled at him. "So now you'll know what to do, and

the next batch will turn out better."

"I don't share your faith in my ability." He glanced at Johnna, who reverently turned the camera over in her hands. "I tell you what, Laurel: I'll pay you forty-five dollars and give you my camera for the pieces I selected."

April and Johnna both gasped.

Laurel shook her head. "Just the camera."

"And thirty dollars."

She'd never seen a camera like this one. It intrigued her. "I'll get just as much enjoyment out of the camera as you do from the sketches—probably more."

"Oh, will the both of you stop haggling like horse traders?" Johnna handed the camera to Laurel. "Only horse traders want to cheat one another, and you're bendin' backward and pussyfootin' 'round, trying to be fair."

Gabe chortled. The sound of his merriment made Laurel let out a self-conscious giggle.

"It's about time the two of you came to your senses and agreed on something," April said. "I want to go on that walk, and you're wasting precious time."

"Meet me in the middle." Gabe looked at Laurel. "Twenty-two fifty and the camera."

"Fifteen and the camera," she countered.

"Are you always this stubborn, princess?"

She merely laughed and nodded.

"Hey, what's going on—oh! Rutlidge!" Paxton and a few others strode up. Pax held up a string of fish. "How about you staying for lunch?"

"I don't mind as long as the cook doesn't."

Laurel smiled. "I'm the cook, and I don't mind at all."

❧

I've been wrong about her. Oh, I was right—she's a princess. Regal and beautiful. But she's more than just appearance. The woman can cook, and her artistic abilities are enough to put her in one of the finest European academies.

Gabe ate the last bite of his trout almondine and wondered who thought to pack almonds with the supplies. "Great meal."

"Our table is always open," Laurel told him.

"Don't say that too loudly. The cavalry is poorly provisioned. They might start ghosting alongside you and showing up for meals."

April shrugged. "They're welcome. I expected the men to be more hungry than usual, so I almost doubled my provisions. We're about halfway through the trip, and we've used about a quarter of what I packed."

"I hate thinking that the men who keep this beautiful place safe for all of us might have to do without." Kate looked up from the girth strap she'd been repairing. Gabe hadn't been able to talk her into waiting until after lunch—she'd been adamant about relieving his "poor little horse" at once. "Can we get word to them? How do we reach them?"

"Captain Wood has a way of finding me," Gabe confessed.

He quelled a smile at the memory of their last meeting. The soldiers were disappointed he didn't have any new food after having been to Wawona, but the licorice pipes more than redeemed him in their eyes. They'd been like little boys, relishing that treat around the campfire.

"Captain Wood," Caleb repeated. Gabe noticed he, Paxton, and Tobias tended to assert themselves as leaders in the group.

"Yes. He's a solid man, a good commander," Gabe attested. "If he or his men show up, you can count on them being well-disciplined and helpful."

"Here. This is done." Kate stood.

Gabe rose. "I'm grateful. What do I owe you?"

Kate gave him a disbelieving look. "Mister, it was nothing to fix. We Chances take care of horses."

"So do I. It was my horse, and you provided a valuable

service. I can't abide with mistreating a beast. I'd have stopped using him as a packhorse if this couldn't be remedied, and that would have put me in deplorable straits."

"So I helped a fellow traveler." Kate shrugged.

"How about if you take the girls on a walk, and we'll call it even?" Caleb swiped his biscuit across his plate. "They've been wanting to explore, and they're driving us half crazy."

Gabe looked at the women. "Do all of you ride?"

"We've grown up on a horse ranch," Laurel reminded him.

"Why don't I take you on a ride? You'll see more, and we could determine where you'd like to walk tomorrow."

"Laurel, take your camera!" Johnna urged.

"Actually, you'd be better off leaving it here at camp and carrying it on the walk. I found my horse had a bad habit of moving just about the time I hit the shutter."

"Makes sense," Caleb said. "You probably tense up a mite, and horses react to the least little signal."

"Then I'll leave the camera here." Laurel brushed a little speck off of her skirts. "We'll be ready as soon as we do the dishes."

"We'll see to saddling up your mounts," Paxton said.

Gabe watched as some of the men went over and prepared four nice-looking mares. Each of the beasts behaved perfectly. The bay with the special saddle had to be Kate's since she loved to do leatherwork. The stockier mount would be for short, plump April. That left the other two—a dappled gray and a strawberry. He couldn't decide which was Laurel's and which was Johnna's. Laurel would look like a princess on the gray, but the strawberry's walk resembled a dainty march.

Peter sauntered over. "I aim to go along. Promised Pa me or one of the boys'd stay with Sis all the time."

"Fine." Gabe glanced at him. "So Johnna's your sister?"

"Yup. Folks named us all after the apostles. John was the beloved disciple, and it's held true. Our Johnna's something special—ev'rybody latches onto her. On account of that, Ma was downright worried 'bout her comin' so far from home."

Gabe watched the women as they washed and dried the dishes. They chattered like happy little sparrows. "From what I see, all the women in the family are extraordinary."

"Uh-huh. April's a fine gal. Nobody cooks better, and she's got a big heart. Kate—well, a feller couldn't hope to have a gal who's a better listener. Laurel's been the surprise. We all expected her to be a pain on this trip. Finicky and scared. Nary a complaint's come outta her. Fact is, last night she told us we've got bears and snakes back home, so she didn't know what the fuss was all 'bout." He chuckled.

I misjudged her, too. In fact, I'm no good at reading women at all. I was just as wrong about Arabella. "Just about the time a man supposes he's figured out a woman, she changes on him."

"Ain't that the truth!" Peter leaned against a tree. "Contrary creatures, but the dear Lord said it's not good for a man to be alone, so I reckon I'll marry up and have to tame one of 'em someday."

"Are you sure you're the one who'll do the taming?"

Peter tilted his head back and let out a loud hoot. "Now that's a poser, it is. I'll exercise my mind on it someday. What 'bout you?"

"Me?" Gabe scowled. "The last thing I want is to have to worry about what a woman wants out of me. Being footloose suits me just fine."

"You made 'em all happy with an offer of a ride."

Gabe merely shrugged. A few minutes later, he walked over and untied the tether on his mount. He prized his horse—a Tennessee Walker he'd bought with his hard-earned pay. Though he came from a wealthy family, his father insisted upon his sons having to work in the business and learn the value of a dollar. The lesson wasn't in vain. Then again, Gabe never regretted a single cent he'd paid for Nessie.

"That's one fine beast you've got there," Paxton said.

Gabe nodded in acknowledgment of the praise.

"You ever breed her?"

"No." Gabe gave the mare an affectionate pat. "I've been too selfish to give up riding Nessie for long enough for her to be in foal. If I ever do, her offspring will be sweet-tempered."

"Back home, we have a couple of stallions who would do her justice." Paxton grinned. "I'm not just boasting. Chance Ranch is known for its horseflesh."

Looking over at their rope corral, Gabe commented, "You have a wide variety. You never specialized in any particular breed?"

"We've got everything from bays and blues to mustangs and pintos. Army buys up a couple of sizable strings each season—enough to keep us in business. The rest go to regular folks—farmers, ranchers, travelers."

"Not a one of your mounts has marks."

"You mean a brand?" Paxton clarified.

"No, lash marks—from harsh discipline." Gabe watched Laurel's brother's face cloud over and hastened to add, "I've seen several horses—the wild mustangs that needed taming—that have gotten the spirit whipped out of them."

"Not at our place." Laurel walked up. "Love works miracles. We care for our horses, and they give us their best."

Kate skipped up. "While we're here, four of the younger boys are getting their horses. In our family, everyone is given a horse when they turn twelve."

"A rite of passage?" Gabe marveled aloud.

"Sort of." Paxton winced and theatrically rubbed his backside. "The boys are given a rough horse and have to break it. If you ask me, the horse makes a man—not the man makes the horse."

"And the girls?"

Laurel smiled. "We're given mares that are already domesticated and saddled."

"Daddy said it's because the Chances protect their women," April chimed in, "but I always said it's because the men would starve if anything happened to the girls."

"I don't blame them. I've tasted your cooking." Gabe grinned. "Are we ready to go now?"

Tobias and Tanner brought over the girls' mares. Gabe managed to be standing by Laurel, so it only made sense that he help her mount up on the dappled gray. "Here you go," he said by way of warning that he'd put his hands on her. The satiny ribbon of her sash felt smooth and cool to the touch, and yards of buttery yellow fabric fluttered as he cinched hold of her waist and lifted.

A gentleman never looked straight ahead or down as he helped a woman into the saddle. Gabe fought the temptation and kept his head tilted back until Laurel gained her seat: then he turned his head to the side and regretfully let go. He heard her fuss with her skirts to be sure her ankles didn't show. He'd forgotten how potent the swishing sounds of petticoats and the fluff of ruffles could be.

"Thank you, Mr. Rutlidge."

"You're welcome, Miss Laurel." He swung up into his saddle and turned to look behind him. "Are you all ready?"

"More than ready!" Kate sang out.

"Please don't hold back on our account," April begged.

"Yeah," Johnna agreed. "Don't mean to sound boastful, but we cain keep up with whate'er pace you set."

Gabe soon discovered they hadn't exaggerated their abilities. He'd originally planned a little half-hour jaunt, but these women wanted far more than anything that simple. They trotted along and called out several questions. Laurel rated as the most curious of them all. She wanted to know what animal different tracks belonged to, commented on the similarities and differences in the flora, and asked for comparisons to other areas of the preserve.

Gabe figured they could have talked nonstop for weeks, but he felt the temperature drop. "We need to turn back."

"Do we have to?" April sounded forlorn.

"We'd better, unless you want to bed down out here in the wilds without fire or a bedroll," Peter responded.

"I've done it afore." Johnna didn't look in the least bit afraid.

"Your brothers will scalp me if I don't have you back soon," Gabe said.

Laurel laughed. "Only because they'll be wanting supper."

"It's best we go back," Kate nudged her mare. "We have to cross that open area, and I want to give Myrene her head. If the sun's setting, I'll be too worried about gopher holes to allow her free rein."

Her mare brushed a low-lying branch, and a few bees took off. Gabe watched them zoom around in angry flight, then circle Laurel. "Don't swat at them!"

"I know better." A moment later, she stiffened and her mare sidestepped skittishly. Air hissed in through Laurel's teeth.

seven

Sting. The word didn't begin to describe the horrid burning Laurel felt. She'd counted three stings, but it might as well have been a dozen for the fiery feeling.

"Laurel?" Gabe brought his horse alongside hers and dipped his head to get a good look at her.

"Oh, no. You're stung," Kate moaned. "I'm so sorry. It's my fault."

"There's prob'ly more where those came from." Peter tilted his head to the side. "Let's move."

Gabe reached over and took Laurel's reins. Thankful, she released them as it allowed her to try to pull the stinger out of her wrist.

"Leave those alone a minute. I'll help you get the stingers out." His voice sounded both firm and calm as he led her horse.

"We have tweezers back at camp," April called back.

Unsure just how far they were from camp since she'd been too busy enjoying the ride to determine whether they'd curved around, Laurel winced. She didn't think she could bear the stingers that long.

"There's a clearing to the right about fifty yards ahead," Gabe directed. "Stop there."

That's not too far. But we won't have tweezers. Laurel clenched her hands together to keep from trying to pull out the stinger.

"Whoa." Her dappled mare obediently stopped at Gabe's command. He dismounted, reached up, and cupped Laurel's waist. "C'mere, princess." He swept her down to earth. "There's a log over here. Let's have you take a seat."

Laurel nodded. Seconds later, Gabe knelt before her. He took a knife from the sheath on his belt. "I'm going to flick the stinger out."

"You'll cut it," Kate objected.

"We always use tweezers back home," April told him.

"I'll use the back of the knife, not the blade." Gabe proceeded to curl his warm, large hand around Laurel's wrist. "Hold still."

" 'Kay."

He pulled the skin taut and did just as he'd promised. The stinger came free, and he brushed it away. "Now where else did they get you?"

"My cheek."

"Oh, lookie. Thar's one on yore throat, too." Johnna sat next to her and took hold of her hand. "Peter, mix up some mud. These gotta smart something dreadful, and hit'll take away that hurt."

Gabe leaned closer and repeated his earlier order, "Hold still."

Laurel barely tilted her head in agreement.

April started to giggle. "I'm sorry. This isn't funny, but it looks like Gabe is shaving you!"

"If you don't hobble your mouth, he can always use that knife to scalp you." Kate plopped down on Laurel's other side. "Pay no mind to her, Laurel."

Laurel closed her eyes and felt cold steel pressed against the burning spot on her cheek. A breath later, the blade was gone.

"Almost done," Gabe said as he tilted her head back and to the side.

Opening her eyes a mere slit, Laurel saw the concentration on his face as he rid her of the last stinger. Once it was out, he gently ran his fingers across her brow, right by her hairline. His touch made her shiver.

"Any more, princess? Do you sting anywhere else?"

"No." Her voice came out in a tight whisper.

"Got that mud here." Peter wedged in.

Gabe dabbed his forefinger into Peter's cupped palm and dabbed splotches on her cheek, neck, and wrist. When Laurel wrinkled her nose, he murmured, "I warned you. I'm not artistic."

"It doesn't look that bad," Johnna declared.

Loyal as could be, April and Kate agreed with vivacious nods.

Gabe rose and again tilted Laurel's face to his. His dark brows knit, and his voice took on an edge. "Now will you stop using that fancy flowery stuff?"

"She has to." April bumped him out of the way and wrapped her in a hug. "We understand."

"Well, I don't."

"Lye soap makes her rashy," Kate explained.

"Makes her look like a spotted owl," Peter tacked on.

"Sorta like that mud does," Johnna added.

This kept getting more embarrassing. Laurel rested her head on April's shoulder and groaned.

Gabe pried April away. "Are you feeling sick?"

Laurel shook her head.

"Light-headed?"

A gasp escaped her. No gentleman ever posed such a question of a lady. Laurel straightened up and drew in a strangled breath. "I—"

Before she could finish her sentence, he'd swept her into his arms and was striding toward his mount. "We're getting you back to camp. Does anyone know if she's ever been stung before?"

"I don't know about bees. She's been stung by wasps," Kate said as she swung into her own saddle.

Gabe handed her off to Peter, mounted, and took her back.

The jut of his jaw screamed grim determination. "Hang on, princess."

The ride from camp had been leisurely, delightful. The ride back amounted to nothing more than a blur and the pounding sound of horses' hooves. Gabe held her tight, and the steady beat of his heart beneath her ear kept her feeling unaccountably safe. The sun was setting as they skidded into camp.

"What's going on?" Pax demanded as Gabe passed Laurel down to him.

"Bees."

Laurel wiggled until her brother set her down. "Really, I'm fine."

"She needs to lie down," Gabe insisted.

"Why?" Pax looked from her to Gabe and back.

"She's sensitive—even lye soap bothers her. She was having trouble breathing." As he spoke, Gabe wrapped his arm about her and started escorting her toward the tent. "You ladies, come tuck her in."

"I'm not sleepy," Laurel dug in her heels. "Other than wearing mud all over, I'm fine."

"Well, if you're fine, can we have supper soon?" Cal patted his stomach. "I'm starving."

"I'll cook," April declared.

"It's my turn," Laurel said.

"They're my fish." Kate headed toward the campfire. "I caught more than the boys did."

"Now there you have it." Johnna grabbed Laurel's hand and dragged her into the tent. "Everything's under control."

Spinning around, Laurel hissed, "You're no help at all. The boys didn't want me to come on this trip because they thought I'd be too much trouble—that I'd fuss and need special attention. The last thing I want is—"

Johnna clapped her hand over Laurel's mouth and whispered

in her ear, "Them bucks out there cain think whatever they please. Better they reckon 'twas jest a case of yore stays being cinched a tad too tight than you havin' hysterics or bein' brought low by a couple of bitty bees."

Unable to refute that logic, Laurel nodded.

"So what we're a-gonna do is spend a moment or two in here, then go back outside and pretend nothin' ever happened."

"Nothing did happen!"

Johnna shrugged. "Ma onc't tole me, a man's gotta think he's right. A smart woman lets him think what he will, and she jest keeps doin' what needs to be done."

"That seems like lying to me."

"Nah." Johnna grinned. "Men use their strength to help women. Seems only fair women exercise kindness in return."

"When you put it that way. . ." Laurel reached up to fix her hair.

Johnna slipped behind her. "I aim to loosen you up."

"I don't need you to. I'm fine."

"Ain't about what you need, Laurel. Think on it: Gabe scooped you up and toted you like you was a damsel in distress. He'll be made to feel like a laughingstock iff'n you sashay outta here."

"Just a minute ago, you said we were going out there and pretending nothing ever happened."

"Shore 'nuff I did. But how're we gonna *pretend* nothin' happened if nothing happened?" Johnna deftly unbuttoned the back of Laurel's gown.

"I could just loosen my sash."

"We'll do that, too."

❧

Gabe stood off a ways from the tent and kept staring at it as he paced. A few of the Chance men had taken the horses and were seeing to them.

Paxton leaned against a tree and folded his arms across his

chest as Ulysses turned to Caleb. Entertainment tinged his voice as he drawled, "It's just a bee sting."

"Three." Gabe grimaced as he paused. "And I've seen a man die from being stung."

"No foolin'?" Ulysses gawked at him.

"He swelled up and stopped breathing."

Paxton straightened up. "And Sis was having a hard time breathing."

"No use getting too excited yet," Caleb asserted. "She was talking plenty when Johnna hauled her into the tent."

"Could be," Ulysses mused, " 'twas a matter of her um. . . whalebones."

"Don't you talk about my sister that way," Pax growled.

"Laurel's never been swoony," Caleb said. "Prissy but not swoony."

"She's not prissy; she's feminine," Gabe snapped. "Enough of this jawing. We need to know how she's fairing."

The tent flap opened. Johnna emerged. Laurel followed right behind. Gabe squinted and studied her. In the lantern light, her coloring qualified as hectic. Her lips. . .if she'd stop chewing on the bottom one, he could see whether they'd swelled at all.

"Sis," Paxton called, "you okay?"

Her hand went to her breastbone, but she nodded.

Gabe stomped toward her. "If you won't lie down, you should at least sit."

"I'm going to help finish supper."

"Not while you're wearing mud." April shook a long-handled fork at her.

"I'll wash it off."

"No, you won't." Gabe glowered at her. "Johnna said it takes away the pain."

Caleb came up on Laurel's other side. "Maybe we ought to trade it for new mud. It might draw off the poison."

"They were bees, not rattlesnakes."

Ignoring Laurel's objection, Gabe nodded. "I'll take her to rest by the fire. You get more mud."

"Is she all swoll up?" Ulysses called over.

Gabe studied Laurel's lips. Since she'd worried them, they'd taken on a deeper tint than usual. They looked okay. No, they looked fine. Real fine. Downright kissable. *What am I thinking?*

"Well?" Ulysses prodded. "Are they?"

"No." Gabe slipped his arm around her waist and started toward the fire. "Grab a wet rag, will you? We need to wash off the old mud pack."

"Sure."

Laurel looked up at him. "This is unnecessary."

Gabe nudged her to sit down. "Let me take a look at those stings." Though she made no complaint, he witnessed how her features tightened as he used the wet cloth to remove the mud.

Paxton whistled under his breath. "Those things've gotta be the size of—"

"Your skin is sensitive, princess," Gabe interrupted. The last thing she needed to know was that the stings had puffed out to the size of a quarter. "But these'll go away in a few days." For the second time, he dabbed mud on her pretty face.

"Don't forget her wrist," Peter reminded.

"Got it." Gabe attended to that one, too. He wished she couldn't glance down and see that huge wheal. Laurel, who loved beauty, would take a good look and worry about being permanently disfigured.

"What are you putting on her?" Kate held a graniteware mug.

"More mud."

She shook her head. "Clean it off. I made a paste of baking soda for her stings."

Laurel grabbed for the cloth. "I'd much rather use the baking soda." As she dabbed at her jaw, her eyes widened.

"Stings swell like that," Gabe reassured her. "It'll go down in a couple of days."

"Days!"

Paxton chortled. "No use kickin' up a fuss, Sis. It's not like we're at home where you'll have suitors knockin' down the door to see you."

Hearing she had suitors shouldn't have come as a surprise. Nonetheless, Gabe didn't like the fact whatsoever. He grabbed the rag. "You missed a spot."

Laurel turned her big amber eyes toward him. "I'm probably wearing mud crumbles all over."

"A little dirt never hurt anybody," Kate declared as she dipped her finger into the mug.

"Cleanliness is next to godliness," Laurel recited.

Johnna walked over with several dinner plates balanced on her arms. "Now's the wrong time to declare such a thang. Ev'rybody here could fill a dustbin with what they shake outta their duds."

"I suppose you're right." Laurel's smile rivaled the lantern for brightness. "I've never felt closer to the Lord than I do here in Yosemite."

Her profession took him off guard. Gabe understood the overwhelming appreciation for the beauty she sensed. *But what does God have to do with it?* No use burdening these people with the perplexing questions he entertained regarding faith. Best he change the topic to something light. Gabe jerked his chin toward Kate and grinned. "Put that baking soda on her and see if she feels closer to the kitchen, too."

Everyone laughed, but deep inside, Gabe felt empty.

eight

After supper, everyone gathered around the fire. As had become their custom, they conversed. A couple of the boys had brought harmonicas and soughed through them softly. Peter brought his fiddle, and about every other night he'd rosin up his bow. Often as not, they'd all end up singing a few songs. One of the men would finally stand and say a prayer to end the evening.

Gabe and Pax wouldn't leave her side. Sandwiched between the pair of them, Laurel resolved to forget about her stings and relish the evening. Bless his heart, Pax might grouse and growl at times, but he was a fine brother. As for Gabe—well, she'd never met a man like him. He'd been strong yet gentle— but though Daddy, her uncles, and brothers were those things, too, with Gabe it was. . .well, different.

He listened and joined in the conversation now and then— most often to make a suggestion regarding adventures the men could enjoy during the remainder of their trip.

Peter fetched his fiddle and played "June-bugs Dance."

Kate called, "Play 'There are Plenty of Fish in the Sea.' "

"She asked for that because she caught the most fish today," Tanner grumbled.

The rest of the men laughed, then began to sing as Peter started to play.

Laurel leaned toward Gabe and said quietly, "Whenever Kate dangles a hook, fish fight to bite it. It drives the boys daft."

"Does she use the same bait?"

"Yes." Laurel wrinkled her nose.

"So you don't particularly like to hook crickets or worms?"

66

She pointed ruefully at her wrist. "Insects and I don't get along."

"I'd rather see you with a paintbrush than a fishing pole in your hand any day of the year."

"This little thing will be gone by the time we reach Bridal Veil. I'll be sure to paint that picture for you."

"Good. Thanks."

When the song ended, Tobias started singing, "For the Beauty of the Earth." Laurel joined in.

On the refrain, Gabe finally added his voice. His deep tone rang true. He turned and smiled at her as he sang the next verse, "Hill and vale, and tree and flower, sun and moon, and stars of light. . ."

His love of their surroundings came through with great sincerity. Though she'd always enjoyed the hymn, Laurel hadn't ever found it this expressive. Bee stings aside, this had to be the best day of her life.

After a few more songs, Pax rose. "Suppose we ought to call it a day. Let's pray. Lord, we want to raise our praise to You for so much—for the wonders of Your creation, the love of family and friends, and the mercies You show us. We give special thanks for taking care of my sister today. Keep us and those we love safe through the night we pray, amen."

"Amen," everyone chimed in, but a mere breath delayed Gabe's, and he was looking at Laurel.

She shivered.

"Are you cold?"

It seemed ridiculous to say yes on such a balmy night and when sitting so close to the fire. Laurel shrugged. "I'll be under my quilt in a few minutes."

"Sweet dreams."

Minutes later as she snuggled in the tent, his words echoed in her mind again. *Sweet dreams. . .*

But when she woke the next morning, Laurel couldn't recall

having dreamt at all. She quietly dressed, put up her hair, and gathered a tablet and her watercolors.

Johnna sat up and stretched. "D'ya ken whether April had special plans for breakfast? I'm hankerin' after biscuits 'n' gravy."

"It can't be morning yet," Kate mumbled.

"Jist 'cuz we ain't got no rooster to crow here don't mean the sun forgot to make an appearance." Johnna reached over and poked at Kate. "You and me—we got breakfast duty. Rise 'n' shine."

Kate opened one eye. "The Bible says the Lord loves a cheerful giver. It doesn't say He favors a cheerful riser."

"Sleep in. I'll help with breakfast today." Laurel set down her art supplies.

"I'm not ashamed to accept that offer." Kate rolled to her other side and dragged her quilt over her head.

Johnna grabbed her clothes and swiftly dressed. In the dim light of the tent, she squinted at Laurel. "Might be a good notion for you to wear your laces a bit loose today. Yore cinched in within an inch of yore life."

"Nonsense. Look. My dress fits the same as it always does."

Johnna shook her head. "For true, you look bitty as cain be. Plenty of men like that to look at; but when hit comes to gettin' serious, a man wants a woman whose shape says she's a healthy 'un."

"I'm healthy as a horse." Laurel hoped the conversation would end there.

April propped her head up on one hand and whispered loudly, "Did you notice she didn't say anything about a man getting serious? I know her too well, Johnna. She's getting tenderhearted over a certain man."

"I thunk so, too."

"You have no idea what you're talking about." Laurel turned to leave the tent.

"He didn't wish any of the rest of us sweet dreams," Johnna said.

"He was worried about me after the bee stings is all."

"She ain't foolin' us. Think she's foolin' herself, April?"

April's giggles filled the tent. Laurel would have gladly dashed out, but if she did, she'd have to explain why her face was so red.

The sound of a horse leaving camp at a trot came through the canvas. Kate sat up and flung off her blankets. "Nobody's letting me sleep. Even the boys are up and rustling around."

"I only heard one horse," Johnna said as she reached for the tent flap. "Hope we don't have us a horse thief."

They bolted out of the tent in time to see Gabe riding away. Johnna shook her head. "Silly man's gonna miss out on biscuits 'n' gravy. Shoulda waited."

Laurel's heart dropped to her knees. *What if he heard what they said in the tent?*

A few minutes later, Laurel dropped the spoon in the gravy as she stirred it. She burned her hand on the coffeepot. How could she ever face Gabriel Rutlidge again after what he'd overheard this morning? After breakfast, she gathered her tablet and charcoals and escaped to the relative privacy of a nearby stand of trees. It didn't help distract her. When the second of her charcoals broke under the pressure she exerted, Laurel slammed the tablet shut and let her head drop back against the trunk of the tree she'd been leaning against.

Lord, I don't know what to do. Back home when boys came to call, it was so easy. I knew them from school and church. But compared to Gabe, they are all such. . .boys. With them, I knew exactly what to expect. Gabe is so different, so wonderful. He understands how I feel about this place. No one else ever looked past the pictures I paint and saw the emotions behind them, but he did. Yesterday, he was so good to me when I got hurt. I didn't want my brother's strength or help; I wanted Gabe's. But Gabe rode off this morning. Did he hear what the girls said in the tent? Will I ever have a chance to get to know him better, or did they scare him off? Was he just being kind yesterday, and I'm making a ninny of myself? I'm so confused, Father.

"Laurel!"

She scrambled to her feet. "Yes?"

Caleb sauntered toward her. "You gals wanted to go for a walk yesterday. You feelin' up to it now, or do you wanna stay here and draw?"

"Oh, I'd love to come along."

"Johnna's hoping you'll take that camera."

She stooped to pick up her supplies. "It's fascinating, isn't it?"

"Yup."

Smothering a smile at the immediacy of his answer, she rose. "Gabe said there are one hundred exposures in the roll. I'm sure we'll all snap a few pictures."

"I'd like that." The light in his eyes tattled that's what he'd been hoping for. "It'd be good to have pictures of the places we've climbed."

"Absolutely. It'll be a nice keepsake, and we can show them to everyone back home so they'll be able to anticipate their trip here next summer."

He bobbed his head affirmatively. "Go shove your stuff in the tent, and we'll get going."

"I made a picnic lunch," April announced as Laurel came into sight.

"How fun!"

Caleb snorted. "We're eating outside for every meal. What difference does it make?"

"We eat outside at home a good deal of the time, too," Paxton tacked on.

"But this will be in a different place," Kate said. "We don't want you boys dragging us back to camp after we've only been out a little while because you've gotten hungry."

"I need someone to hang the food for me." April finished knotting the top of a sack. She looked at Ulysses. "If a bear gets to this, you boys'll have to make your own lunch."

"Whoa. I got it." He snatched the bag and headed for the rope dangling from a high branch.

Laurel tucked her tablet and charcoals into the crate in the tent, then grabbed the camera. Turning the black device over in her hands, she wondered how to operate it. *Gabe was supposed to stay here today and take us on this hike. He would have shown me how to take photographs.*

April ducked into the tent and whispered, "It's getting hot. I'm shucking one of my petticoats."

"You are not, April. That's indecent."

"Mama lets me wear just two at home in the summertime."

Shaking her finger, Laurel whispered, "That's at home. This is out where someone might see you!"

"Like who?" April started to shimmy out of a row of white cotton ruffles.

"Yesterday Mr. Rutlidge showed up."

"He couldn't tear his gaze off of you and your pictures long enough to notice anything else in the world." April opened her trunk and shoved the petticoat inside. "And don't bother to deny it. I'd give up dessert for a month to have a man look at me that way."

Kate romped in. "Did you do it?" She stopped cold as a guilty expression crossed her face.

"Laurel told me not to, but I did anyway. Your skirt is dark. The sun won't shine through it, even if you're only wearing two. Go ahead," April urged.

"Kathryn Louise Chance," Laurel said, "when your mother was your age, she wore all three petticoats and every other proper layer even in the unbearable heat of the tropics."

"She was a missionary's daughter and had to serve as an

example. I don't have to be an example. Besides, that was in the olden days."

Johnna tromped into the tent. "What's the hold up? Sun's gonna set afore we ever walk away from this here campsite."

"I don't want these girls out there unless they're decently attired."

Johnna pursed her lips. "I don't see nuthin' wrong."

"Laurel wants us to wear all three petticoats," Kate complained.

"Land o' Goshen." Johnna's eyes widened.

Oh, good. She'll talk sense into April and Kate.

"I've only been wearin' two the whole livelong trip. Ain't nobody seen anythin' wicked 'bout it, so I don't get what the fuss is about. Just shake a leg, else our brothers ain't gonna set aside any more days to take us on hikes!"

Shoulders drooping, Laurel waited for her cousins, then left the tent. *How can everything have gone so topsy-turvy?*

nine

"Hey, Rutlidge!"

Gabe halted Nessie and turned in the saddle. Dust churned under the hooves of the cavalry horses as the men rode across the distance to join him.

"Where's your packhorse? You camped nearby?"

"Not too far." Gabe hesitated for a moment. He'd already mentioned the cavalry to the Chances. They'd been more than clear about the welcome the men would receive. Then again, Gabe didn't exactly want these men around Laurel. *The girls. I mean the girls,* he quickly corrected himself.

"Thing have been quiet," Captain Wood said. He stretched in the saddle. "I'm going to veer us up toward the pastureland and oust the sheep again. Thousands of those dumb animals, and they're eating all the vegetation the indigenous animals need."

"Shore could tolerate a good mutton roast." One of the soldiers yanked on his uniform coat. "Need somethin' to keep my slats apart."

"I think we can do something about that," Gabe said.

"Oh?" Captain Wood grinned. "Did you go get provisions?"

Gabe shook his head. "Met up with some folks who are camping out here."

"They got extra grub?" The soldier perked up.

Gabe directed his words to the captain. "They're good people. You and your men can count on plenty to eat tonight."

"Lead on," Captain Wood ordered.

An empty campsite lay before them when they arrived. Gabe looked around, and the only signs of life were some squirrels frisking through the branches and pesky blue jays pecking at crumbs beneath the table. All of the horses were gone, and not a soul stirred. Thinking the girls might be in the tent, he called out, "Hello!"

No one answered.

Gabe didn't want to dismount. He'd not think to enter someone's home when they didn't answer the door, and tramping through an empty campsite felt like the same invasion. The fact that he'd brought ten uninvited guests only added to the strain.

"Hey. Ain't just men campin' here," one of the soldiers said. "Men don't bother with clotheslines or fancy stitched dish towels."

"They're ladies," Gabe gritted. "And you'll treat them accordingly."

"My men wouldn't think to do otherwise," Captain Wood said. He then ordered, "Dismount."

In short order, two men set up a rope corral a ways off from the one the Chance men had established. Gabe still hadn't dismounted. "River's that way. I'm going to water my horse."

The cavalrymen were in the process of mounting up when Ulysses came riding up with a long string of horses behind him. "Howdy!"

"Ulysses."

"Fine looking horses. I'm Captain Wood."

"Good to meet you. Ulysses MacPherson. They're Chance horses. None finer."

Gabe dismounted and helped Ulysses get the wet horses into the corral. "Looks like they played as much as they drank."

"That's a fact. Hot as it is, I reckoned they might like a swim in addition to a drink." Ulysses grinned. "Kept me from havin' to haul any water, too."

"Where are the others?"

"Most of 'em went on a hike. They're itchin' to try out that camera. Couple of the boys and me—we lazed around today. I left 'em at the river to swim off some dirt. Johnna told me afore they left this mornin' that iff'n the boys didn't clean up today, they wouldn't get fed tonight."

Gabe nodded. "I can hear her saying that. About dinner tonight. . ."

Ulysses squinted as he surveyed the soldiers. "I reckon these men are ready for decent vittles. Livin' in the saddle don't allow for carryin' any extras."

"You said it," one of the men agreed.

"Why don't y'all unsaddle and take yore horses for a swim?"

Captain Wood didn't crack a smile, but his voice took on an entertained tone, "Are you inviting our horses or us to supper?"

"Horses cain take care of 'emselves." Ulysses folded his arms across his chest. "But I ain't a-gonna account for what my sis'll say 'bout me lettin' scruffy men come to the table when she made that threat afore she left."

Gabe saw to his horse and made good use of a bar of soap. He hurried at the river, not wanting any of the men to get back to camp before he was there to watch out for Laurel and the girls. When he reached camp, Tanner and Paxton were hiking in from the other side. "You're back," he said.

Tanner nodded. "I could say the same thing. You took off early this morning."

"Yeah, I did." Gabe shrugged. He wasn't accustomed to informing others as to his whereabouts. "Where are the girls?"

"Driving Packard, Caleb, and Peter crazy, lollygagging along."

"Are they tired? Do I need to take horses to them?"

"Nah. They've gotta stop every five minutes to gawk." He caught sight of the new rope corral and saddles heaped by it. "I met up with the cavalry."

"I wondered when we'd cross paths."

Tanner's bland acceptance left Gabe feeling better. If the women took the dinner guests half as well as the men did, things would be fine. *Then again, the men don't have to do the cooking. . .*

Gabe went to the fire pit. The park allowed visitors to chop and use deadwood, and someone had a good-sized stack of wood available. Kindling, logs, and his flint, and he started a fire. "Tanner, where are the coffeepots?"

"Couldn't say. Suppose I could dig 'round for 'em."

Ulysses pointed toward one of the buckboards. "They've been keepin' dishes and such in the crates on the back of that 'un. Tanner, why don't you tote some buckets down to the river. Send the boys back with 'em, and we'll start up a few pots."

A short time later, Kate's voice sounded from a distance. "Oh, I smell coffee!"

The men had been sitting around, jawing. Gabe and the cavalry all shot to their feet.

As soon as they rounded a bend in the path, Peter said, "Gals, looks like we got us some visitors."

"Really? Who?" April wiggled up beside him.

"United States Cavalry, miss," Captain Wood announced.

"You soldjer boys hungry?" Johnna asked.

"Yes'm." The enthusiasm behind that male chorus left everyone grinning.

"If you'll excuse us for a moment," Laurel said, "we'll freshen up and start cooking." She slipped into the tent.

Gabe walked to his saddlebag, then headed toward the tent. "Laurel?"

She stuck her head out of the flap. After a day of hiking, her hairpins had all skidded around, leaving her bun loose. Wisps of dark hair spun in tiny curls, framing her face. "Yes?"

All of a sudden, Gabe felt ridiculous. He'd gotten up early this morning and ridden clear to Wawona and back to buy these for her. But she needed them. He shoved two bars of soap at her. "Here. Use this. It won't attract insects like your other stuff."

She reached out and accepted them. "Thank you." Looking down at them, she said, "Ivory. Oh—I've heard of this. It's supposed to be very mild! Thank you."

He nodded. "It floats." *Why did I say that? I'm blathering like an idiot.*

"How fascinating!"

April walked up. "Soon as we freshen up, we'll have dinner going. I already put on the rice to boil. Hey—Ivory soap! I heard those bars don't sink."

"Let's find out." Laurel's smile at him made the whole trip worthwhile. "Thank you for your thoughtfulness."

"It was nothing."

❧

"Mmm. That was something," one of the cavalrymen said.

"There's plenty more," April said. "Help yourself."

"Don't mind if I do." He rose.

The captain handed over his mess tin. "Seconds for me, too." He turned back to April and Kate. "Best order I've given all week."

"These women can cook." Gabe's arm brushed against Laurel's.

The contact made her want to lean closer—as if it were possible. They were all crowded around the campfire. An enormous pot of rice sat on the table next to two other pots— one was empty now; the other soon would be, by the way the men ate with such gusto.

"April gets the credit." Laurel set down her fork and patted her cousin. "She's amazing in the kitchen."

"You all worked on the meal," Gabe said.

"It was nothing." April stirred the food on her plate. "It all came from cans and boxes."

"Nothing we ever make turns out like this," one of the soldiers grumbled.

"It's just canned chicken, a box of dehydrated vegetables, and Borden's condensed milk." April shrugged.

"And broth and seasonings," Kate tacked on. "You just dump it over rice."

Gabe forked up a bite. "Sure beats beef jerky."

"Anything is better than that," Laurel agreed.

"Somethin' else is ticklin' my nose," one of the men said.

"Yeah. Here. Hang onto this, will ya?" Johnna shoved her plate into his hands and knelt by the fire. Using the hem of her skirt as a hot pad, she turned a Dutch oven halfway around.

"I'll get this one." Laurel rose, and Gabe reached out to take her plate. She smiled her thanks, handed it off, and rotated the second Dutch oven.

As she took her seat and accepted her plate, Gabe's brows rose in silent question. "Dessert."

The right corner of his mouth kicked up. "I figured that much out. You ladies wouldn't let us near the table while you prepared it, so we're all wondering what it is."

"I say, we let 'em wonder awhile longer," Johnna said. "Pa always put for the notion that a man ought to be happy with what's on his plate and trust the Lord for whate'er would come next."

"Your daddy must not have had to survive on his own cooking for any length of time," one of the cavalrymen shot back.

Johnna wrinkled her sunburned nose. "Actually, my pa and two uncles et their own cookin' for a handful of years."

"Then when he said he trusted the Lord for whatever came next—assuming their cooking was anything like mine," Gabe said, "he must have meant whether they'd wind up with food poisoning."

While the others laughed, Laurel turned to him. "Your cooking is that abysmal?"

"Worse. I even manage to burn oatmeal and corn mush. I wouldn't mind learning a thing or two."

"I'd be happy to teach you."

"Great." He tilted his head toward the Dutch oven. "How about if we start with that stuff?"

"Mr. Rutlidge! Were you trying to play on my pity to make me reveal what's cooking?"

His eyes twinkled. "I'm wounded that you'd ask such a thing."

"He might be wounded, Sis," Pax said wryly, "but he's not denying it."

"I thought we were friends. Friends don't keep secrets."

Laurel couldn't hold back her giggles anymore. "Shame on you, Gabriel Rutlidge!"

"I'm shameless when it comes to good food. You have to take pity on me and all of these other men. We've been subsisting on our own cooking for so long, our taste buds went into hibernation. A grand meal like this jolted them awake."

April lifted both hands in surrender. "I can't stand it anymore. It's cobbler."

"Arghhh!" Johnna let her head drop back.

Kate clapped with glee. "I knew it!" She turned to Johnna. "Told you!"

Johnna nodded. "I'll do the dishes tonight."

"No, you won't." Gabe hefted another large bite. "You gals cooked up a feast. I'm willing to wash. Which of you men'll dry?"

"You're offering to wash dishes?" Laurel blinked in surprise.

"Sure. Why not?" He filled his mouth.

They managed to demolish all of supper and both apple cobblers. Laurel didn't know what to do with herself as men did the dishes. What was happening? Back home, the men never did dishes. For that matter, neither did the boys.

"Livin' on their own, I s'pose these men're used to takin' care of thangs," Johnna mused. "Shore is odd, seein' 'em do women's work."

Laurel nodded. "It makes me sad to think of them serving our country and eating so poorly. Let's plan a special breakfast."

Peter brought out his fiddle. One of the soldiers wheeled around. "A dance!"

Laurel and Johnna exchanged surprised looks. Before either could respond, Gabe barked, "No."

ten

Paxton, Caleb, and Peter were only a breath behind in the denial.

Gabe cleared his throat. "These ladies don't dance, but they sing like angels. Perhaps you could ask them for a song."

"We'll have a sing around the campfire," Caleb announced.

At suppertime, the soldiers had all vied to sit beside the women. Laurel noticed how her brothers and cousins managed to elbow their ways into sitting next to their sisters now. She wished Gabe could sit beside her again, but she said nothing.

After the second song, he sauntered over. Though a large man, his gait was nearly silent—yet she sensed his presence. He slapped Packard on the shoulder.

Pack twisted around. "Done with the dishes?"

"Yep."

Pack stood up and wandered over to the other side of the fire. Gabe took his place. He looked over her head at Paxton and held his gaze for a long moment, then glanced down at her and smiled.

She stumbled over the lyrics of the song and recovered, but for the rest of the evening, Laurel could barely contain her elation. Because her uncle Titus loved to play guitar so much, they often sang in the evening back home—but with her mother and five aunts as well as the younger boy's high voices, the harmony stayed balanced. With twenty-odd men and only four girls, the air vibrated with deep notes. Gabe's voice carried a rich timbre that warmed her clear down to her toes.

They sang "Oh! Susannah!" and "I Dream of Jeannie with the Light Brown Hair," then "Laura Lee." Kate tossed a little chip of wood into the fire and said, "You can tell the girls are outnumbered here. The men all keep suggesting songs with girl's names. Let's sing a hymn."

Gabe winked at Laurel and cleared his throat. She got the feeling he was up to some kind of prank. "What about 'Beautiful Valley of Eden'?"

"Oh, I like that one." Kate beamed. "It's more than fitting for where we are, too."

One of the soldiers chuckled. "I have a sister named Eden."

"My aunt's name is Eden, too," Gabe confessed.

"You're a rascal." Laurel ruined her scold by laughing.

"We should make him pay a forfeit," April declared.

"I concur," Captain Wood said. "Discipline is vital. The punishment should fit the crime. I recommend he sing that hymn solo."

Gabe rose. Folding his arms across his chest, he widened his stance. "Laurel shares the guilt. She knew I was up to something."

Her jaw dropped at his audacity.

"Then they'll sing a duet," the captain declared.

Extending his hand to her, Gabe invited, "M'lady."

Paxton nudged her. "Get going, Sis."

"I'm protesting my innocence." She took Gabe's hand and stood.

"Methinks the lady doth protest too much," Ulysses called from the other side of the fire.

"Oh, you and your Shakespeare," she said back.

"Beautiful valley of Eden!" Gabe began singing. He squeezed her hand.

She joined in, *"Sweet is thy noontide calm. . ."*

Peter didn't accompany them; they sang the hymn a cappella. Gabe didn't turn loose of her hand, and Laurel didn't pull away. Somehow, it just felt right for her hand to be enclosed in his strong, warm grasp. The unity she felt with him went beyond the blending of their voices—they were sharing the love of God and His wondrous creation. So much else felt topsy-turvy in her world, but this felt as solid and secure as anything she'd ever known.

❧

Gabe woke to the smells of fresh coffee and wood smoke and the hushed whispers of women's voices and swishing skirts. He lay in his bedroll and relished those simple things. All around him, the Chance men and the cavalry formed blanket-covered lumps on the ground. The warm summer night hadn't required a fire, so they'd scattered about and bedded down after last night's music.

Gabe noted the Chance men had all managed to plop down closer to the tent than they had in the past. To his knowledge, there hadn't been any discussion about it—but there hadn't been any last night, either, when the horseman suggested a dance. These men showed a protectiveness that pleased Gabe. He didn't want Laurel or her cousins to be in any danger.

Not that the soldiers were dangerous. It had been an innocent suggestion last night—but Gabe didn't want those men spinning the women around and wearing them out. Back home, plenty of churches frowned upon dancing. Gabe wasn't sure where the Chances stood on that issue. Even if they considered it harmless, he figured a woman ought to be well acquainted with a man before he took her in his arms. He'd not even taken Laurel's hand into his until last evening. There was no way he'd allow any other buck to sweep her around to music.

The Chance men aren't the only ones being protective. He lay there and identified his Laurel's sweet voice as she and April discussed the breakfast menu. *My Laurel? Mine?* He heaved a sigh. *Who am I kidding? I'm not just being protective; I'm being possessive. That gal hasn't tried a single coy move, yet she's beguiled me.*

But I don't want to get roped into any woman's world. Yosemite is my refuge. I need to back off and let this be a friendship. I can appreciate her company and artwork. When she leaves, she'll go back to her well-ordered world, and I'll still be free to roam at will. It's for the best.

He rolled over onto his side and opened his eyes. Peter MacPherson lay on his side, facing him. He inhaled deeply and rasped, "Ain't nuthin' better'n the smell of coffee in the mornin'."

"I agree."

"Ma always wakes Pa up with a cup. One of these days, I'm gonna find me a good woman who'll do the same for me."

Gabe crooked a brow. "That's pretty specific. Do you have a mere mortal in mind?"

Peter chortled and sat up. "I might, but I'm not sayin'. In my family, a man learns to keep a few things to himself. If he don't, he'll niver live past the teasin'."

Gabe sat up, shook out his boots, and yanked them on. "To my way of thinking, I'm better off to wake up and make my own coffee."

"Good Book says 'tisn't good for man to be alone." Peter stomped his foot to make it fit into the boot.

"Yes, but then God made Eve for Adam—a perfect fit. Adam didn't hold a question in his mind that they were intended for one another. The rest of us men—we have lots of women to choose from, and we don't have that same assurance of finding the perfect fit."

Peter shrugged. "I reckon no couple is a perfect fit at the start—it takes years of bumpin' along to rub each other smooth."

Gabe rose and folded his bedroll. All around him, men were waking and rising. All of them offered an opinion on marriage—all but Caleb seemed to think it was something far off in the future.

"Shore, some of you bucks are too wet 'hind the ears to do any courtin'," Johnna said. "And you soldjer boys ain't home, so no gal's gonna want a man who's married to his saddle. Others of you—well, I'm thinkin' God'll have His way sooner'n you expect. I'm gonna have me a good laugh when you get moon-eyed over some purdy l'il gal and change yore tune."

"She's saying that because she has Trevor wrapped around her little finger," Peter said.

"Watch what yore sayin'," Johnna said. "Trevor's goin' o'er to our place and holpin' with some of yore chores so's you could come on this trip."

"She's got you there," Pax teased.

Ulysses snapped Peter with his blanket. "Face it: Trevor's doing it so your ma and pa'll find favor with him. He's buildin' up the nerve to ask for Johnna's hand and figures it's smart to get on their good side."

"Ma and Pa only have a good side." Johnna shook a long spoon at them. "And Trevor's got a helpful spirit. Hit ain't worthy of you to fix motives to him."

Peter brushed by Gabe and muttered, "See? Toldja in my family, a smart man keeps his mouth closed."

"It's not just in your family—it's a sound rule for any man."

Gabe's resolve to keep his mouth full of food and empty of words lasted only until breakfast was ready. Plate heaping with flapjacks and bacon, he sat in the same place he'd occupied last night. When one of the cavalrymen came over to take the seat beside him, Gabe clipped out, "Miss Laurel will be sitting there."

"Then I'll sit on her other side."

Gabe nodded curtly and shoveled a bite in his mouth.

Five minutes later, Laurel walked away from the serving table with a plate of flapjacks. The cavalryman called out, "Miss Laurel, we've been saving a place for you over here."

Gabe couldn't decide whether to be embarrassed or grateful for that outburst.

Laurel smiled as she sauntered over. "I thank you, but I'm not ready to eat yet. We made plenty of the flapjacks. Would you care for more?"

"Don't have to ask me twice." The man's plate shot out, and Laurel expertly flipped two sizable flapjacks onto it.

She looked at Gabe.

"They're great. Thanks." He held out his plate and accepted a pair. "But I don't feel right about eating when you haven't yet."

Laurel smiled. "I'm rarely hungry in the morning. I often skip breakfast and stay out sketching or painting." She wended her way past a few more men and soon emptied that plate. After refilling the plate, she continued to serve seconds.

Kate wandered along in her wake with a jug of maple syrup and poured it for whoever wanted more, and Johnna did the same with coffee. April stayed by the fire, continuing to cook.

Caleb strode over and straddled a log by Gabe. He bent over and seemingly checked out the frayed hem of his britches as he asked in a low tone, "Do you think the captain would be offended if we offered some of our provender? We have plenty to spare."

"I'm sure he'd be grateful."

"You going to travel with us awhile, or do the girls need to set aside some grub for you, too?"

I'll be leaving as soon as breakfast is over. The words were right on the tip of his tongue. Gabe couldn't make any other decision. Only the syrup made the answer stick to the roof of his mouth, and once he washed it down with a gulp of coffee, he heard himself said, "Where are you going next?"

❧

"What do you have there?"

Laurel didn't turn at the sound of Gabe's voice. She'd

sensed his presence a few minutes ago. In the past week while he'd been camping with them, he always showed his thoughtfulness for her work by waiting silently until her brush or charcoal lifted from the paper. As she dabbed a tiny splotch of dark green on a tree, she said, "Another landscape. I must have painted hundreds of them since I've been here."

"Every one of them is beautiful in its own way." He moved to stand beside her.

"Thank you. As the weeks have gone by, I'm noticing the colors I use are changing. I'm using more dark green instead of the lighter tones. It's been a subtle shift, but the difference is still there."

"I don't doubt it. Springtime green is more yellow-y." He looked into the distance, then back at her picture. "It's the same, but it's not. How do you decide when to leave out a clump of trees like you did right there?"

Tilting her head to the side, she thought for a moment. "I knew I was doing it, but I didn't give much thought as to why. Now that you ask, it's because the picture would feel lopsided with more over here." She indicated where the trees belonged with the wooden tip of her brush.

"So you balanced it out."

She nodded. A slight breeze lifted the edge of the paper.

Gabe reached over and whistled under his breath. "When did you do this?"

"First thing this morning." She waited a second for the watercolor to finish drying, then leafed back for him to see the whole piece. "They were so beautiful."

"So the doe had twins. From what I've seen, that's quite common."

"I was afraid they'd move before I could capture them." Laurel looked at the sketch. "I'd like to paint them when I get home."

"It'll make a stunning picture."

She touched up one spot on the sketch. "I didn't know twins were common in deer. They don't happen much with the horses on our ranch, and when they do, the men practically pull their hair out."

"The foals don't survive?" Gabe asked softly.

"Daddy counts it a blessing when the mare and one of the foals survive. I can only think of three sets of twins that made it through."

"That's a pity."

"Kate's mare was a twin. Neither the mare nor the other foal survived. Our neighbor brought her over in hopes that my father and uncles might be able to get another mare to accept her. None of them would, but Kate hand-fed that foal and pulled her through. The only time I've ever seen Kate cry was that Christmas when her mother and father told her they'd bought the horse so she could keep it."

"That must have been when she was twelve."

Laurel gave him a surprised look. "How did you guess?"

"You mentioned once that the kids in your family receive a horse when they're twelve."

"You have a good memory. They're breaking the rule this summer. Cole, my youngest brother, is eleven. He and three of the others who are ten and eleven are all getting a horse. The plan is for them to master their animal so they can ride them here to Yosemite next summer."

Gabe straightened up. "So you'll be returning next year?"

"No." She sighed. "I'd love to, but we made a deal. The group that came this year will stay home and run the ranch next year while our parents and the younger kids come."

"That's some arrangement. Do you think you'll all be capable of keeping the place going?"

"I've thought about that." She flipped the tablet to a new sheet. "Grandma and her sons started that ranch when the boys were our ages. If they could do it, we can. We also have the MacPhersons next door, and they'll bail us out if we run into anything we can't handle."

"You're not afraid of hard work."

"Why should I be? God's blessed us with health and meets our needs. My aunt Lovejoy says it's only right that we meet Him halfway by baking that daily bread."

Gabe shifted his stance and looked away for a moment. "I wondered how you're set for supplies. I'm thinking of riding to Wawona to send off mail."

"April's the one to ask. She's kept track of the food."

"I meant art supplies, Laurel."

"Oh."

"I can't have you run out. Bridal Veil is next."

Mixing water in with the paint to lighten the tone of blue for the sky, she frowned. "I looked all through that store and don't recall seeing any tablets or pencils."

"I called that to Hutchings's attention the last time I was there. It never occurred to him to keep them in stock, but once I mentioned it, he promised to get some in. So—what do you need, and do you have any mail you'd like to send out?"

"Would you mind waiting while I write a quick letter? I'm sure others would love to send word home, too."

"That all depends."

She started to swirl her brush in water to rinse it out. "On what?"

"Your definition of quick." He plucked the glass from the easel and handed it to her. "My mother's idea of a short letter is ten pages." Collapsing the easel, he tacked on, "If that's your plan, I'll already be halfway to Wawona."

"I thought your horse was named Nessie. To make that kind of distance, you'd have to be on Pegasus."

"You've never seen her in a full-out run."

"Who's running?" Tobias asked.

"I am." Gabe started back to camp. "I aim to go to Wawona today."

"Any special reason why?"

Laurel gawked at her cousin. "Tobias, don't pry."

"I don't mind." Gabe shrugged. "They have a telephone there. It's my mother's birthday. I thought I'd give her a call."

"They have a telephone here?" Tobias marveled.

Unable to contain her amazement, Laurel asked, "Your mother owns a telephone?"

Gabe hitched a shoulder as if it were nothing.

"We don't even have telephone lines going through Reliable yet. I saw a telephone when I went to San Francisco this spring, but that was in a huge mercantile."

"I'll bet they're a lot more common in the big cities back East," Tobias mused.

Gabe scanned their surroundings. "The government was wise to set aside this national park. I hope they're smart enough not to let the modern world intrude. It would spoil the natural beauty to have a tangle of telephone lines, paved roads, and electric lights here."

"I can't see that happening." Laurel shook head. "The big cities barely have a touch of those things. It wouldn't make sense to run those services out this far."

"I dunno." Tobias grinned. "I saw a string of those electric lights in Sacramento. They make for an astonishing sight."

Gabe leaned the easel against the tent. "I'll take starlight over Yosemite over Broadway's Great White Way any night of the year."

"You've been to New York City?" Laurel squeaked.

"I've done a considerable amount of traveling."

"Have ya now?" Johnna tilted her head. "Like where?"

"Today, I'm going to Wawona." Gabe grinned at her. "I told Laurel I'd be happy to mail off letters, but you only have a little while to write them. You'd best get busy."

Caleb perked up. "Someone gimme some paper. I want to write to Greta."

April handed over some paper and teased, "After you're done giving her all of your love, tell her I love her, too."

A few minutes later, Paxton and Packard sauntered up to Laurel. "Give Mom and Dad our love, Sis."

She leveled them with a glare. "Each of you sit down and write at least a few lines."

"Aw, Sis—"

Pax looked downright smug. "Didn't bring any paper."

"Aren't we lucky I have plenty." Laurel handed each of them a piece of her stationery.

Packard shoved it back at her. "I'm not writing on paper that's all girly."

"Me, neither."

Laurel accepted the violet-bedecked stationery. "Okay." She paused for a moment, then pasted on an oh-so-innocent smile. "You may each take a sheet of my art paper. It's plain as can be, so I'm sure it won't offend your masculine sensibilities."

Paxton huffed and headed for the tablet still hanging from the easel. Packard stayed put and gave her a taunting grin.

"Did you need something?" Laurel asked.

"Nope. Just remember what Mom always says: 'Be careful what you ask for.'"

"What is that supposed to mean?"

"You want me to write, I'll write. . .just a few lines." His gaze shot off toward Gabe, then back at her. "I'm sure Mom and Dad will be very interested." He shoved his hands in his pockets and whistled as he walked toward Paxton.

Laurel stared at her brother's back in horror. Packard could be teasing, but he could also be telling the truth. Only what his version of the truth would be. . .well, that was unpredictable. Pack accepted a sheet of paper from Paxton and said something.

Paxton threw back his head and bellowed out a laugh.

"Yore brothers are up to no good," Johnna said as she took a place across the table from Laurel.

"At times like this, I remember why I was so glad the Chance girls have their own cabin." Laurel stared at her stationery and tried to figure out what to write. She'd planned to mention Gabe in her letter—now, she'd have to be careful what she wrote. Not knowing what her brothers intended to say only made it worse.

"You gonna let yore folks know a handsome young buck's brought you a courtin' gift?"

"What?" Her head shot up.

"Gabe brung you that fancy soap. Made a special trip just to fetch it for you." Johnna bobbed her head. "You done turned his head. Night after night, he sits a-side you. I reckon yore brothers'll spill the beans iff'n you don't."

Laurel leaned across the table and whispered, "Soap is not a courting gift."

"Thank what you want." Johnna shrugged. "Mind iff'n I use one of them fancy sheets of paper you brung?"

"Here." Laurel passed her several and pored over her letter. She'd already waxed poetic about the beauty of Yosemite and remarked on how well she'd taken to camping. Mentioning how the boys all went on climbs and she'd been drawing and painting ought to have been enough—but now, it wasn't.

What should I say about Gabe? If I say too much, Mama will read between the lines. If the boys make this out to be a courtship and I barely give him mention, Mama's going to have a conniption.

Steeling herself with a deep breath, Laurel started to write again. *We met an interesting gentleman named Gabriel Rutledge. He's spent considerable time in Yosemite and gave us invaluable information so we have been able to use our time wisely. One night, he brought the cavalry to camp with us! He's spent a little over a week in our company now, and I traded some of my drawings for his Kodak camera.*

There. She'd devoted a whole paragraph to him. Not that it said much. But she really couldn't find anything more to say that wouldn't cause problems. *The truth of the matter is, I don't know how to explain how I feel. I barely know the man. I don't know what he does for a living, but I know how much he loves nature and Yosemite. He likes art and horses—and I know deep in my heart he likes me. He's kind to the other girls, but he's different with me. It's thrilling. But it's scary, too. He's from a big city back East. I never want to live anywhere but Chance Ranch. Nowhere else could ever feel like home.*

Johnna tapped her pencil on the tabletop and sighed. "Tryin' to describe what we've seen is harder'n talkin' Pa outta the last piece of rhubarb pie."

"You can tell them it's all breathtakingly beautiful, and we've taken photographs."

Perking up, Johnna nodded. "That'll tickle 'em sommat fierce. We'll have genuine photographic pitchers to show 'em onc't they come back from gettin' de-veloped. I'll say you're paintin' up a storm, too. Thataway, they cain see what we've seen, and I don't have to trouble myself o'er trying to put hit all into words."

"I don't mean to be rude, but I'm going to rush you folks." Gabe started to saddle Nessie. "I plan to set out for Wawona in just a few minutes."

Laurel quickly scribbled, *I can't thank you enough for my easel. It's been wonderful. Mama, you'll want to borrow it when you come here next year. I love you dearly and miss you. God be with you all.*

"Anyone have an envelope?" Caleb waved his letter to Greta in the air.

"I brought several," Kate called back. "Come and get 'em."

Peter walked over and peered over Johnna's shoulder. "Tell

Ma and Pa that I love 'em."

She flipped the paper over. "Write it yoreself." She flashed a smile at Laurel. "Hit'll mean more iff'n it comes from his own hand."

Laurel nodded as she folded her sheets and slid them into the envelope.

"Lookie thar. You already put a stamp on the envelope."

Handing Johnna another stamped envelope, Laurel smiled. "I can't take credit for that. It was Mama's idea."

Peter finished scribbling a few lines and set down his pencil. "Yore ma's done a fair share of travelin'. I reckon hit's one of them things she learnt along the way."

"Your mother travels?" Gabe asked as he walked up.

"In her younger days." Mama was still sensitive about having been a gambler's daughter with the attending footloose lifestyle. Though Laurel loved her mother and was proud of her, she didn't mention the cause out of respect for Mama's feelings. "Now Mama is content to live on the ranch and tend her garden. The only time she leaves is to go to San Francisco for her art shows."

"You'll have to hold a show of your own," Gabe said as he accepted letters. "But I get first pick before anyone else touches your pieces."

"You've seen everything she's done since she's been here," April pointed out.

"The trip's not over yet." He looked about. "Any more letters, or is this it?"

"Here's mine." Kate galloped up and handed hers to him. "Laurel, do you know what your brothers did?"

Dread iced her spine. "What?"

eleven

"Aw, c'mon, Kate," Pack moaned.

Kate folded her arms akimbo. "You tell her, or I will."

"I don't want to know!" Laurel blurted out. After Packard's threat earlier, she couldn't imagine having him embarrass her in front of Gabe.

"I do," Ulysses said.

A chorus of "Me, too's!" sounded.

Pack and Pax exchanged a look. Laurel felt heat creeping from her bosom to her hairline. When slow, rascally smiles quirked their mouths, she wanted to dive under the table.

Pax cleared his throat. "We. . .uh. . .used your art paper, like you said we could."

"They used pictures, not blank pages," Kate snapped.

"Just little ones—like a picture postcard," Pack hastily added. "You know the old saying—a picture is worth a thousand words. So I just wrote, 'This is where we are. Having a good time.'"

Laurel slumped and let out a shaky sigh.

"You what?" Gabe thundered.

Pax shrugged. "She's got hundreds of pictures. She won't miss a few."

Brows knit and face dark, Gabe widened his stance. "Your sister has a gift. You respect it."

"Gabe, thank you for liking my work—but it's okay. Really." Laurel patted his arm. "I should have thought to include pictures. Mama and Daddy will love to get a peek at what we're seeing. I don't begrudge my brothers a few little pictures."

95

Pax nodded. "Chances share."

Laurel flashed Gabe a smile. "Since it's your mother's birthday, why don't you choose a picture and mail it to her?"

He didn't even blink. "How much for the one you did of thc poppies?"

"It's a gift!"

"I'm giving it, so I'm buying it."

"The man could teach stubborn to a mule," Johnna declared.

"Well?" Gabe prodded.

"Eggs," April said. "They have to be expensive up here, and we're almost out."

"Yes." Laurel gave him an exultant smile. "A dozen eggs. Can you get them?"

"You sell yourself short."

"You've never tasted April's sticky buns. She needs eggs to make them."

"Whoa." Peter wound his arm around April's shoulders and gave her a squeeze. "You'd make sticky buns?"

"I will if Gabe pays for Laurel's poppy picture with eggs."

Peter looked at Gabe. "I'd take it as a personal favor if you'd agree."

Laurel popped up. "I'll go get that picture."

Gabe halted her by wrapping his hand around her wrist. "Only," he said as he looked at everyone, "if Laurel gets first pick of the sticky buns."

Paxton slapped him on the back. "Being around us is rubbing off. We just might make a Chance outta you."

"You're going to scare him off," Laurel said.

Gabe crooked a brow. "Not a chance."

❧

Balancing the keg across his thighs, Gabe rode back to camp. This was the second time he'd brought back a load of eggs. Packing them in straw this time was a whole lot lighter; last time, cornmeal buffered the precious eggs.

While at Wawona, he'd run into the Kibbies, who lived in the far northwestern portion of the park. They were some of the few legal residents of the land. Mr. Kibbie saw Laurel's picture of the poppies and fell in love with it. Unwilling to part with it, Gabe asked Laurel to make another. He'd ridden north from their current campsite by El Capitan to exchange the picture for more eggs.

Yesterday, he'd climbed El Capitan with six of the men. Today, the others were climbing with Caleb and Tobias's guidance. He had to give the Chances and MacPhersons credit; they never left their sisters on their own, even when they ached to explore.

Since he'd joined up with them, Gabe had put himself into the rotation to stay with the girls. It was supposed to work out to be every third day—but in actuality, he often helped plan a day's events to include a ride or hike in which the women could participate.

As he approached the campsite, Gabe looked at all the clothes fluttering on the line. His own spare shirts and britches hung among them. Since coming to Yosemite, he'd taken to swimming in his clothes to wash them. That technique worked well enough; but after yesterday's climb, they were filthy. Laurel had turned a fetching shade of pink when she told him to be sure to leave his laundry in the pile with everyone else's.

"Hey, Gabe!" Kate called to him as he drew closer. "There are still a few good hours left. Want to go fishing?"

"No." April shaded her eyes and looked up at him. "We don't need fish for supper."

"No use catching what we don't need," Gabe agreed as he ducked under the clotheslines and came fully into view.

Johnna's eyes narrowed. "That's some git-up you've got on 'round your boots."

"Johnna!" Laurel set down the shirt she'd been mending.

"Well, it is. Take a gander."

"Better still, how about you ladies unstrap me?" Gabe glanced off to one side. "Mrs. Kibbie thought you might appreciate some fresh cream. I put a marble in each jar, thinking the ride here might agitate it enough to churn a little butter, too."

"That was clever." Laurel reached up to take the keg from him.

"I'll hang onto this. If I swing my leg over Nessie, we're liable to lose cream, so I'll have to ask you to unwind the strips holding the jars to me." He kicked out of the stirrups, and the marbles in the jars rattled.

Kate started in on his right calf; Laurel bowed her head and began to work on his left. Kate grew impatient with the knots, pulled a pocketknife from her apron, and cut the jar loose while Laurel patiently plied the knots and let the cloth come free. Frowning, Kate remarked, "Those are some of the finest boots I've ever seen, but you need to take care of them. They're awful sorry-looking. Want to use some of my saddle soap?"

"I suppose I ought to. I'll be wearing freshly-washed clothes, so I may as well get cleaned up from tip to toes." He dismounted and settled the keg on the table. "April, I'll gladly polish your saddle and shoes if you'll make more of those sticky buns. You have plenty of eggs here."

"They're best when made with cream." She cast a quick look at Laurel. "But I might have to fight with my cousin for that. She's started to freckle and was bemoaning the fact that we didn't have any buttermilk here to fade them."

"Ever hear of anything so silly?" Johnna pried the lid off the keg. "Kate 'n' me've got a bumper crop of freckles. Neither of us never did a thang to banish 'em."

"Freckled or not, you're all lovely women."

Johnna shrugged. "I reckon if God put 'em thar, they b'long."

Laurel wrinkled her nose. "You and Kate were made with freckles. I'll believe God put yours there. Mine? I can't hold God responsible because I didn't wear my sunbonnet."

April let out a theatrical moan and made a shooing motion with her hands. "Gabe, run while you can. They're about to get into a theological discussion about God doing things or allowing stuff to happen."

"You mean you all don't agree on everything?" He stepped back. "I'm not trying to poke fun. I'm just surprised."

"We agree on the foundational truths," Laurel said. "But when it comes to some of the details, we interpret things differently."

"Happens all the time," Johnna declared. "Parson Abe back home said we cain let those opinions tear apart our church or we cain respect how each of us follows the Lord accordin' to the dictates of our hearts."

"When you boil it all down, the important thing is that we all belong to the family of God through the redeeming blood of Christ Jesus," Laurel said.

"Good. Now that you agree on that, I'm sending you back to your mending, and I'm making sticky buns." April started to roll up her sleeves.

Gabe found a shady spot, accepted Kate's saddle soap, and set to work. The girls chattered as they mended, but he purposefully turned the other way. He had a lot of thinking to do.

Back home, everyone at church was alike. He'd never once heard anyone accept the possibility of someone believing in the same God but viewing Him differently. God was God—unchanging, all-powerful. That much made sense. *And Jesus came to be a peacemaker because men messed up. That's what Laurel meant about the foundation. I agree with all of that. But*

I'm still not like them. They believe it, and it makes a difference in their lives. Me? Those things are just facts.

"I can't decide whether to love you or hate you." Ulysses plopped down.

Gabe looked up from the boot he'd been rubbing.

"You brought eggs, so we're getting sticky buns. You coulda stopped there. But since you're tending your leather, the girls all think the rest of us ought to, too."

"I see." Gabe worked on another deep scuff.

Tanner plopped down next to Gabe and yanked off his boots. "I hear it was your idea for us to polish our boots." He glowered at Gabe. "They're going to get messed up again as soon as we put 'em back on."

Peter joined them. "I reckon we could all jist go barefoot. Ever notice in Genesis, when Adam 'n' Eve figgur out they're nekked, they make clothes, but there ain't no mention of shoes?" He stretched his bare feet out and wiggled his toes. "I'm thankin' God loves us too much to 'spect us to cram our poor feet into boots all day, ev'ry day."

Ulysses whooped and tossed a rag at Gabe. "Don't look so s'prised. You seen us walking 'round the campsite barefoot."

"I thought you left your boots here to keep them dry when you went down to draw water or bathe."

"Nah. Think on it: Shoes oughtta be for protection. When we're workin' or climbin', it makes sense to wear 'em. 'Round the house, a body ain't got cause to box in his feet."

Tanner knocked the dirt off his shoes. "They're not kidding. The MacPherson kids wear shoes in the winter and to church and school, but until they're old enough to do barnyard chores, nobody makes them wear shoes. Go over any evening in the summer, and the whole clan is barefoot."

"Nothin' beats walking in fresh grass. Always makes me think on the Twenty-third Psalm 'bout God letting me lie down in green pastures and leadin' me a-side still waters."

Peter nodded to himself. "It restores my soul."

Caleb wandered over. "Talk about restoring your soul. Could you believe the view from the top of El Capitan?"

"So you're back." Gabe looked up at him. "How did today's climb go?"

"Great!" Caleb grinned. "I took 'em up the exact same route you led us on yesterday. I'd climb that every day of my life if I could, just to have five minutes of the view. Someday I'd like to bring Greta here and let her see it, too."

"I've spent my share of time, standing atop all sorts of places here." Gabe let out a long, slow breath. "Being up there does something inside—the majesty of this place never fails to move me."

"Same feeling as kneeling at the altar," Tobias said.

I don't see how that can be. But I've never knelt at the altar, either.

twelve

"April," Gabe called from the knot of men over on the edge of the campsite, "I'm ready for your shoes."

"They won't fit you," she called back.

"Don't bother her," Peter said. "She's making sticky buns."

"He knows she's making sticky buns," Laurel told him. "He brought the eggs for them and promised to polish her shoes and saddle if she made a batch."

"Well, now, that changes thangs." Peter grabbed Gabe and hauled him over to the cooking table. "April, give up yore boots, or we'll take 'em off of you."

"This has nothing to do with you, Peter MacPherson." April turned away from him.

He grabbed her waist, spun her around, and lifted her onto the table. "Guess again. I aim to do one of the boots and stake a claim on some of them sticky buns."

Caleb elbowed his way over. "Take your hands off of my sister." He tilted her face up to his. "I'm doing the saddle, and I get first pick. Now give up your shoes."

"I already promised Gabe first pick." April couldn't stop laughing.

Laurel stood back and watched as the men all put on a show about squabbling over April's shoes and saddle so they could have more of her sticky buns. Though sweet as could be, April never managed to attract men or be the center of attention—and for once, she'd landed in the middle of their interest. Even if it was just her brothers and cousins, her blush tattled about how much she enjoyed it. Laurel decided to add to the fun. "Nobody's going to want the sticky buns if she messes with her shoes. You'll have to take them off for her."

"Laurel!" April shrieked.

"Well, you have flour all over your hands," Laurel said.

"No use protestin' modesty, neither. We all seen yore feet when you went wading," Johnna added.

"You boys get on with it." Laurel pulled on her apron. "April needs to hurry up and finish with those so I can start supper."

Caleb untied one of her boots and handed it off to Peter. Peter held it up. "Where's the rest of this boot? Looky how dinky this thang is."

"Well, it won't take us long to polish them," Gabe decided.

"You brought the eggs. You did your share." Tobias grabbed for the other.

Laurel laughed at Gabe's nonplussed expression and explained, "There'll be enough for everyone to have two, but there are always a few extra."

Gabe snatched the boot from Tobias.

"Hey!"

"I've tasted April's sticky buns." Gabe clutched it to his chest. "They're enough to make any man greedy."

"You're getting dirt ground into that shirt. It's expensive material, too." Johnna shook her head. "You men jest don't know how much quality fabric costs."

Gabe glanced down. "This would be about eight cents a yard in the East; eight and a half cents a yard on this coast."

"How did you know that?" Laurel asked.

"You mean he's right?" Ulysses gawked at Gabe.

Gabe shrugged. "Family business."

"Well, that makes me feel a whole lot better," Kate blurted out. "I've been worried about you."

"Worried?" Gabe's brows rose.

"Well, we couldn't come out and ask you what you do. You

said you'd been loafing about Yosemite since springtime."
Kate cleared her throat. "I couldn't make it all add up."

"You never asked."

Caleb folded his arms. "We don't. Code of the West is that
a man might have shrugged off his past and deserves a clean
slate. No one pries."

"I see." Gabe's brows knit for a moment. "There are
things I wish weren't part of my slate, but they're nothing
I'm ashamed of. My family owns a textile business back in
Boston."

"Who's running it if you're here?" Tobias wondered.

"My brother, Stanford. Actually, before I left, I sold my half
of it to him."

"You left a family business? Why?" Paxton looked at him in
disbelief.

"I grew to hate it. I didn't want to choke myself wearing a
tie all day long while dealing with people who told bald-faced
lies just to make a better bargain. Almost all of the people in
the community judge one another based on their financial
worth. Stanford finds the whole affair rather amusing; I didn't
want to be a part of it."

"So yore startin' out with a clean slate out here." Johnna
nodded. "I cain understand that. Now you menfolk git back
to yore boots. Dinner ain't gonna make itself."

"What're we having?" Calvin asked.

"Ham and seven-bean soup." Laurel started draining the
water off the beans she'd put on to soak that morning. "Biscuits
and honey."

"You were going to teach me to cook," Gabe said.

"I already mixed and soaked the beans." Laurel plunked
the cauldron onto the table. "If you add a gallon and a half of
water to this, it'll be about right."

"But you can't touch a thing until you change your shirt.
No dirt around our food," April said as she hopped down

from the table and started to sprinkle cinnamon and sugar on the dough.

Half an hour later, Gabe gave Laurel a boyish grin. "Cutting out biscuits with a glass is fun. I never imagined it was this easy."

"You're great with a cup." She smothered a smile. "But I'm not going to praise you for how you handle a rolling pin."

"That contraption hated me."

"Well, you practically snapped it in half."

"I was showing it who's boss." He started arranging the biscuits in the bottom of the greased Dutch oven.

"Oh, is that what you were doing?" April asked in an oh-so-innocent tone.

Gabe surveyed the pans of sticky buns she uncovered and muttered, "I'd say that no one likes a show-off, but in this instance, I'd be lying."

"Hey, Gabe." Tanner sauntered over. "Looks like you're the new biscuit expert."

"Don't say that until they're done baking and you've tasted one."

"We voted and decided to pull up stakes in the morning and head for Bridal Veil." Tanner paused and surveyed the table, then gave Gabe a cat-that-swallowed-the-canary smile. "That means you need to bake tomorrow's biscuits tonight."

"I'll take care of that," Laurel hastened to say.

Gabe looked at Laurel. "*We* will. You measure, I'll mix. You roll, and I'll cut."

Kate turned around from stirring the soup. "Johnna's already taking clothes off the line. I'll go help her pack up our stuff. Do you want me to leave out anything special, Laurel?"

"Not that I can think of." She let out a sigh.

"What's wrong?"

She gazed up at Gabe. "I'm glad to go on to Bridal Veil. From what you've said, I've been anticipating it a lot. I just hate the whole production of packing and pulling up stakes. Everyone's short-tempered on those mornings."

He nodded sagely, then ordered, "Don't do anything with these biscuits. I'll be back in a minute." Striding over toward Paxton and Caleb, he announced, "I have an idea."

April looked over at the men. "Gabe's getting flour all over his sides from propping his hands on his hips."

Johnna's arms were full of laundry, but she halted by the girls. "Puts me of a mind when Pa used to dust the babes with talc. Ended up a-wearin' more'n they did." She smiled. "Gotta like a man who ain't afeared of holpin' with the kitchen or the kids."

"Sis!" Caleb called. "How long before you'll have the sticky buns ready?"

"Twenty-five minutes," April called back as she started to put the first pan over the fire. "Why?"

"Gabe came up with a plan."

Gabe bustled back over. "We need to rush these biscuits. The men are going to pack everything they can, and half will travel on ahead to Bridal Veil. They'll pitch the second tent and set up camp. With the sun setting so late, it'll work. The rest of you will follow tomorrow at a more leisurely pace."

"Where will you be?"

He smiled at Laurel. "I'll go ahead, then come back and meet you in the middle."

෧

"Oh, your plan worked wonderfully." Laurel rode into the new campsite at Gabe's side. "It's so nice to arrive and have the fire ring set up."

He nodded. "Some of the more seasoned scouts do that for wagon trains." He nudged Nessie into Laurel's dappled gray to force her to turn to the side. All day long, he'd waited to see Laurel's reaction to the view he'd revealed.

She didn't move or make a sound. Nessie stepped forward,

and Gabe peered under the brim of Laurel's sunbonnet. Eyes wide and shimmering like pools of gold, she stared at the waterfall. Her mouth changed from a perfect O into a beatific smile. Unable to tear her gaze away, she reached out, touched his arm and whispered, "I've never seen anything this splendid."

He looked at the delighted flush on her cheeks, the delightful freckles speckling the bridge of her nose, and agreed, "I've never seen anything this splendid, either."

"Laurel!" Johnna hollered. "Lookie thar! Ain't that purdy 'nuff to make the angels weep?"

Laurel nodded.

Gabe leaned toward her. "Where do the MacPhersons come from?"

"Next door," Laurel said in a vague voice.

He chuckled. He'd never seen anyone so enraptured.

She turned toward him. "What's so funny?"

"I'm glad to see you're not disappointed in Bridal Veil."

Kate pulled up. "I know, I know. She's besotted. Johnna and I'll cook dinner. Go ahead and get out your sketchbook."

Laurel turned to her cousin. "Thank you."

"If," Kate tacked on, "You promise to do a sketch for our cabin. Don't you think it would be wonderful to hang a picture of that view by our back window?"

"I'm not going to be a gentleman." Gabe looked at her. "You'll have to wait your turn because Laurel promised to paint a watercolor of this for me."

"You all plan to sit ahorse for the rest of the day?" Tobias called over.

Gabe slid out of his saddle and helped Laurel dismount. Kate didn't wait for assistance. He gathered the reins. "I'll tend the horses. You ladies take a few minutes to get your bearings."

In no time at all, Laurel set up her easel and went to work.

Absorbed in her art, she seemed oblivious to everyone's actions. All around her, the Chances were pitching the second tent, cooking, and hanging provisions from the trees. Her focus remained on the waterfall and on her easel.

Laurel didn't join everyone for the meal. April fixed her a plate, and Gabe swept it from her hands. "I'll take supper to her." Staying away from Laurel had taken all of his resolve, but he didn't want anything to disturb her. He wanted this picture to reflect what she saw. By now, she'd be close to done. It always fascinated him to watch as she put the finishing touches on her pieces.

"Ready to eat?" he asked quietly.

"Just a minute." Her hand moved deftly. "Okay." She started to rinse her brush.

"Step aside, sweetheart. Let me see."

Laurel moved.

It was his turn to fall silent. Gabe studied the watercolor in the waning light and knew he'd never be able to part with it.

"If it's not what you had in mind for your mother, I'll—"

"I want it. For myself. I've never considered myself a greedy man, Laurel, but I'm keeping this for my own and asking you to do another for Mom."

"You admitted to being greedy yesterday when it came to April's sticky buns."

Gabe grinned at her. "I've lived a deprived life. Twenty-four years without the culinary or artistic masterpieces of the Chance women. You aren't going to hold it against me, are you?"

She took her plate from him. "I suppose it would be churlish for me to be that way when you brought me supper."

He picked up his own fork and ate a bite of beans. "What do you women do to these? My beans never taste like this."

"Do you add molasses?"

"No. Just a lump of brown sugar if I happen to have some."

"Molasses is what makes brown sugar brown." She smiled. "When we go, I'll be sure to leave you a jar."

Gabe scowled. "Are you eager to go?"

thirteen

Laurel gazed off at the distance. "I miss my family, but I'm not ready to leave here. Chance Ranch has always been home, yet in my heart, I feel—this may sound silly—but from the moment I saw this place, I felt as if I'd come home."

"It's not silly. I understand. Since I arrived, I've felt Yosemite is where I belong."

They finished eating in companionable silence. Once done, Gabe offered, "I'll carry your easel back to your tent."

"Thank you. Here. I'll take your plate."

The next four days were the happiest of Laurel's life. Gabe rarely left her side. He kept her company as she sketched and painted to her heart's content. They rode or walked to several vantage points and took picnic lunches along. When they were alone, he'd call her sweetheart, and at night, by the campfire, he'd hold her hand.

Her brothers and cousins cast her entertained looks. At night in the tent, the girls teased her—but Laurel didn't mind. Gabe spoke of coming to visit Chance Ranch. Her heart soared.

Nothing had been said yet, but when they would break camp tomorrow, she assumed Gabe would ride along with them as they traversed the remainder of the park on their way home. They wanted to spend every precious moment they could together.

"Ready?" he asked after breakfast as he led their horses up.

"Yes." She hung a bag filled with her pastels and a sketch pad to her saddle.

"Up you go." He gave her waist a quick squeeze before

lifting her into the saddle.

They rode about a mile away—within sight of the camp. Gabe was always mindful of her reputation, and Laurel appreciated that he'd not tried to pull her behind a tree and kiss her as some of the boys back home had attempted. She'd always felt a kiss should be something special between an engaged couple, and he'd not yet asked Daddy for permission to court her.

From the way Gabe acted around her and her brothers, Laurel felt sure he was bound and determined to pursue her. Her brothers obviously approved of him. Mama and Daddy would, too. He was honorable enough not to profess his love for her—but his eyes and the way he attended to her testified to of the depth of his devotion. Mama always said waiting for the right man would be well worth it—and she'd been right. Gabe made Laurel's heart sing.

"How's this spot?" He halted the horses near a patch of grass. "Or would you rather be in the shade?"

"This is lovely. I brought my hat, so the morning sun is fine." She accepted his help in dismounting and for a brief moment, he drew her to himself in a tender embrace.

"I don't want to let you go," he said.

"I don't want to go," she whispered back.

He sighed and turned loose of her. In no time at all, they sat together on a blanket. Laurel sketched the waterfall and surrounding landscape, then turned her attention on Gabe. Her pencil moved over the new sheet, forming his general outline and features.

"Hey, what are you doing?"

"Dabbling." She bit her lip and continued. Capturing the essence of a person always challenged her. The slightest tilt of the head, the crook of a smile—the very nuances that conveyed personality made all the difference in the outcome. Other portraits she'd done had been for fun, but this one mattered.

She wanted a picture of Gabe. Very few photographs were left on the camera, and she'd only taken one of him.

"Stop drawing me and do a self-portrait. I need one of you."

"I have a hard enough time drawing others. Drawing myself would be impossible."

"Use a mirror."

"It doesn't work that way." She continued to work on her sketch of him. Concentrating on his eyes, she said, "A portrait has to reflect the personality of the subject. I notice the little details like the impish gleam in eyes or the odd habits like walking with fisted hands. It's what makes a portrait look authentic, and I don't notice those things about myself."

"I'd take whatever you drew."

"You're not very picky." She used her gum eraser and rubbed out the edge of one of his eyebrows. "I'm not good at portraits, anyway."

"I disagree. I've seen the ones you've done of your brothers and cousins."

Shaking her head, Laurel asserted, "I'm better at nature— landscapes, flowers, animals. When it comes to humans, I'm mediocre." She glanced up at him and smiled. "I try to console myself with the fact that God started out with nature and man was His greatest creation."

"So you'll get better with practice?"

She shook her head. "Not appreciably. It's one of those things where I decided that though I want to be as much like my heavenly Father as I can be, that's one of the areas where I'll simply bow to His majesty."

"How do you do that?"

Laurel shrugged, "I try to concentrate on the areas where He gave me talent."

"No, that's not what I meant." Gabe looked at her intently. "I mean, how do you figure out what He wants of you? How do you bow before His majesty?" His brow furrowed. "It's all so nebulous."

"It's not always easy to determine what His will is and follow it." She drew in the details of the collar of Gabe's shirt and the buttons.

"Laurel."

Something in the tone of his voice caused her to set aside her pad. "Yes?"

"You and your family talk about God differently. I don't get it."

"What's different?"

He shrugged. "I can't put my finger on it. I go to church. We say grace at mealtime."

"Those are things you *do*," she said slowly. The conversation took her completely off guard. "Anyone can behave that way—they're actions. When God calls us to *be* Christians, we're to have a change of heart that transforms us."

"How do you hear Him when He calls?"

Laurel stared at Gabe and tried to disguise her utter surprise. All along, she'd assumed he was a Christian. He knew all of the hymns by heart. He was respectful at prayer time.

"Is something wrong?"

Yes, her heart screamed. *I've fallen in love with you, but you're not a Christian!* Laurel moistened her lips and prayed for wisdom. Finally, she looked at Gabe and invited, "Why don't you tell me about your relationship with the Lord?"

Gabe tented one knee and propped his bent arm against it. He thought for a moment and heaved a sigh. "I don't know. I mean, I guess I'm a Christian. I go to church. The other day when you said it all boiled down to thinking Jesus saved mankind from sin, I figure it's right. As for all the things you say about God and creation—I never really stopped to think about Him being responsible, but it had to get here somehow. So since I agree with you about God being the Creator and Jesus being the Savior, then we see eye-to-eye on the foundational matters."

Laurel's heart ached as he spoke. *How can I explain to him that logic and reasoning aren't the same as faithful acceptance and obedience?*

"It's just that all of you act. . ." He shrugged. "I can't describe it."

"We each have a personal relationship with the Lord. It's not just rational acknowledgment of the fact that He exists; we've made heartfelt commitments."

Gabe studied her intently.

"God created us with a need to commune with Him. He walked with Adam each evening in the Garden of Eden. When we sin, we separate ourselves from Him. There's an empty space in us until we are reconciled to Him through Christ Jesus. I think what you sense as a difference is that those of us who have accepted Christ and allowed Him to redeem us no longer seek to fill the void in our lives—He fills it to overflowing."

"My life is full."

Looking at him, Laurel asked softly, "Is it really?"

"Yes." He nodded emphatically. "I've never been happier than I am now. Between coming to Yosemite and meeting you, my life couldn't be any better."

"I appreciate the compliment," she said sadly. "But that's not enough."

"That doesn't make sense, sweetheart." He looked thoroughly confused.

"You want to walk by sight; I live by faith. You're looking for rock-solid proof, and I listen to my heart."

He lifted his hand in a what's-the-difference gesture. "I don't see that as such a problem. Even you said folks can believe differently and still get along. Isn't there some verse somewhere about all the different parts of the body? I guess you're the heart and I'm the brain."

"But when you accept Christ as your Savior, there is a transformation that takes place. You put off the old man and are renewed in His spirit. What difference has He made in you?"

"Why should there be a big change? I grew up in a home that taught values. I know the Ten Commandments and abide by them. Not to sound proud, but I'm a good man, Laurel. I thought you believed that."

"You are a good man, Gabe. I've never met a man as honest and kind and capable—"

"Then what's the big deal?"

She looked down at the sketch she'd made of him. Touching it, she said, "I can draw or paint something that looks just like the real thing."

"Yes, you can. I admire that to no end."

"But it's still lacking something—it doesn't truly have the dimension, the spark of life." She looked at him. "Until we do as Christ said, are born again in the Spirit, we are missing that spark. To have Him dwelling within us gives life a completely new dimension and depth."

Gabe stared at her, but she knew he didn't comprehend what she was saying.

"I can use all sorts of tricks—by shading and using different lighting and colors, I can make a picture appear to have depth. But those are just illusions. You can attend church and sing hymns, pray, and live a virtuous life, but those are just representations, like a piece of art."

He reached over and brushed the tears off her cheeks. "Why are you crying?"

"You're missing the most precious thing in life. It breaks my heart."

"Sweetheart, I'd do anything in my power to make you

happy. I can't lie to you, though. All of this baffles me. If it's a matter of me promising to read a Bible or something, I'd do it; but you said it's not just something a person does."

So shall my word be that goeth forth out of my mouth: it shall not return unto me void, but it shall accomplish that which I please, and it shall prosper in the thing whereto I sent it. The verse in Isaiah went through Laurel's mind. She grasped Gabe's hand. "If I leave my Bible with you, do you promise to read it each day?"

"I wouldn't know where to start, but if you give me some advice, I will."

"Okay." She thought for a few minutes. "What about starting with a Psalm each morning and reading through the New Testament at night?"

He shrugged. "Fine. Only I already know all of the stories."

Laurel squeezed his hand. "Don't read the Bible like it's a collection of stories, Gabe. Why don't you read it like you're trying to get to know Jesus? Study what He does and says as if you were. . .interviewing him to be a business partner?"

He grinned. "That's a novel approach. I can see how it would make me look at Him in a different light." He reached up with his free hand and cupped her jaw. "So is everything better now, princess?"

Reaching up, she curled her fingers around his wrist and pulled his hand back down. Holding both of his hands, she looked into his eyes and barely managed to whisper, "No."

fourteen

"No?" Gabe scowled. "What's wrong?"

Her beautiful eyes filled with tears again. "I. . .made a terrible mistake."

"What's that supposed to mean?"

"I let my feelings get ahead of me. You're so special, Gabriel."

"I feel that way about you, too, Laurel."

"But I can't let this go any farther. We aren't supposed to judge one another, but I did just that. I watched you and assumed you were a believer. Until you give your heart and soul to Jesus, all I can give you is my friendship."

"Friendship?" The word tore from his chest in a low bellow. "I'm way past feeling like a friend to you. I—"

"No." She halted the words by pressing her shaking fingers to his lips. "We're going to be apart from one another. We both have a lot of thinking to do. I know deep in my heart what the Lord's will is. I trust you to do as you promised—to read the Bible and study the character of Christ."

"But what does that have to do with you and me—with us?" He laced his fingers with hers and held tight.

Laurel bowed her head. "We haven't spoken about a future. Forgive me if I misspeak, but there's more to love than just the blending of two hands and hearts." She seemed to struggle to find the right words. "For Christians, the blending of their souls is the most important thing of all. You and I—we couldn't ask God's blessing if we weren't of one accord."

"Hold on a minute. It's not like I'm one of those Chinese

Buddhists or anything foreign like that. I told you: I agree about God and Jesus."

Laurel looked up at him. He couldn't interpret the emotions shimmering in her eyes. "You agree in your head. Let's see after you read the Bible if you agree in your heart."

He didn't want to let her slip away. Given time, Gabe felt sure he'd be able to allay her concerns. Rather than allow her to walk away and close off her heart completely, he grasped at the one chance she'd left open. "I'll read, princess. Every morning and evening."

That evening, she handed him her Bible. He studied the worn leather at the edges and gave her an amused look. "Well-used, huh?"

She nodded.

"I'll make sure I keep up the tradition."

Laurel gave him the first smile she'd summoned since their discussion that afternoon. "Thank you."

"Hey, Sis!" Paxton hollered.

Laurel turned. "Yes?"

"April's begging to stop for a while tomorrow so she can wade in Bridal Veil Creek."

"I'll fish while we're there," Kate volunteered.

"We'll have to set out earlier than we planned to do that." Pax rested his hands on his hips. "So you need to pack up what you can now so we can load up some stuff tonight."

"And I thought he was going to ask us to make the biscuits tonight," Gabe murmured.

"I heard that," Johnna singsonged. She merrily announced, "Gabe just volunteered to help bake biscuits tonight!"

Rather than have their usual nighttime campfire, they all worked to get chores done in advance. Standing alongside Laurel and making biscuits was bittersweet—they did so well together, yet he sensed a gulf between them that he couldn't bridge. As Gabe fell asleep that night, a tune kept running through his mind. He told himself it was just that they hadn't had time to sing as they usually did, but the lyrics to "God Is My Strong Salvation" played over and over again.

At dawn, Gabe got up after a restless night. He took Laurel's Bible and stalked off for some privacy. She'd recommended he start reading in Psalms. *Psalms. I always liked them. David was quite a man. He loved nature the way I do.* Gabe settled down, leafed toward the middle of the Bible and located Psalms.

Blessed is the man that walketh not in the counsel of the ungodly. . .

Gabe jolted at the contents of that short chapter. It didn't mince any words. Flat-out, it compared the righteous and the unrighteous. Laurel was like the third verse—like a tree planted by water. Gabe got the prickly feeling he didn't quite measure up. The fifth verse said sinners shouldn't stand in the congregation of the righteous. *That's what Laurel was saying yesterday—that we don't belong together if I'm not standing right with the Lord.*

Gabe shut the Bible. Everyone at the campsite was already stirring. He went back, took care of his bedroll, and got his horses ready. They all paused briefly for hot coffee, cold biscuits, and a slab of ham. Gabe helped lift trunks and crates into the buckboards, then drew Laurel off to the side.

She wore her pale pink dress—his favorite. The silly thing was far too fancy for camping, but the ruffles and color suited her. Her sunbonnet hung down her back, and the ribbons pulled a little at her slender throat. Her brows winged upward over her eyes, showing slight surprise. She'd never been more beautiful.

Gabe couldn't resist reaching up and playing with one of the tiny curls that wisped by her temple. "Sweetheart, I'm going to leave you today."

Her eyes darkened with pain, and her mouth opened slightly, then shut. She bowed her head.

He tilted her face back up to his. Tears shimmered in her eyes, turning them to molten gold. The sight nearly brought him to his knees. "I read the Bible this morning."

The corners of her mouth bowed upward, but she was still blinking back tears.

"I'm going away on my own to do some reading and thinking." He cleared his throat. "Until I make some decisions, it's not right for us to be together. I can't help how I feel about you. I don't want to help how I feel about you. Believe me, doing the right thing hasn't ever been this hard."

"I–I'll pack you some food."

"No need. I have the supplies I originally rode in with."

To his everlasting surprise, Laurel went up on her tiptoes and brushed a fleeting kiss on his cheek. "God go with you."

❧

"They're home!" Cole shouted over by the barn as the wagons pulled in.

Laurel wearily accepted Daddy's help to dismount and gave him a hug. Mama hurried over and enveloped her in a hug. "Oh, we missed you!"

"We missed you, too," Laurel said. All around her, brothers, cousins, aunts, and uncles were embracing and slapping one another on the shoulder. They'd always been a demonstrative family, and after such a prolonged absence, the emotions flowed freely. But Laurel tried hard to keep her emotions in check. The past five days had tested her to the limit.

"Sis!" Perry yanked on her skirt. "You've gotta come see my horse!"

Laurel smiled down at him. "Tell you what: I have one last picture on a real Kodak camera. I'll take your picture sitting on him."

"Wow!" He wheeled around and shouted, "Cole! My sister

gots a camera. She's gonna take my picture on Siddy."

"I wanna pitcher of me on Quartz!" Cole yelled.

"City? What kind of name is that for a horse?" Pax asked as he grabbed their little brother and swung him in the air.

"His real name is Obsidian, but I call him Siddy. He's black."

Caleb finished giving everyone a hug, then mounted his horse again. "I'm going to see Greta."

Aunt Miriam yanked his sleeve. "Not until you wash up."

"Not 'til you see my horse," Cole protested.

Uncle Gideon looked up at his son. "Caleb, family comes first."

Obviously peeved, Caleb dismounted. "Greta is going to be family—even if you're making us wait forever."

Wanting to cover the awkward silence, Laurel reached into the basket in the buckboard to fetch the camera and said, "I only have one picture left. You young men will have to all line up together with your horses."

As the boys scrambled to comply, Laurel glanced around. Chance Ranch still looked the same, but it felt different. The little boys had turned into—well, not men, but they'd matured significantly. The ranch had always seemed so big, and as ranches went, it was; but compared to the enormous vistas of Yosemite, home felt. . .snug.

"I can hardly wait to see your drawings and paintings," Mama said. "The ones the boys sent home are enchanting."

Daddy nudged up on Laurel's other side. He dipped his head and rumbled, "But we want to hear more about this Rutlidge fellow."

Laurel almost dropped the camera. As soon as she took the picture, Daddy swiped the camera from her, shoved it into Packard's hands, and steered Laurel toward his cabin. Mama had hold of her other arm.

"What did Laurel do?" Craig asked loudly.

"Hush," someone said as her parents marched her up the porch and shut the door.

Laurel wilted into the nearest chair. Daddy paced until Mama stopped him. He turned and glowered at Laurel. "Did that scoundrel steal your heart?"

"He's not a scoundrel."

Mama's eyes narrowed. "But your heart—"

Knotting her hands in her lap Laurel said sadly, "I love him. He's a good man—just ask any of the boys."

"So you're just upset at leaving him behind," Mama said in a tentative tone.

Laurel shook her head. "He knows about God; he just doesn't know God. It's all a rational thing to him. He goes to church and sings the hymns, but—"

"Oh, Laurel," Mama groaned.

Daddy sighed. "Honey, you know better than to keep company with a man who isn't walking with the Lord."

She nodded. "As soon as I realized it, I drew a line." She paused and tried to swallow back the ball in her throat. Her nose and eyes stung from trying to hold back the tears. "But I was too late. I left my Bible with him. He promised to read it."

Daddy came close and pulled her to himself. Laurel rested her cheek against his shirt and gave in to the need to weep. When she finally calmed down, Daddy handed her his bandana. She wiped her face and held the soggy cloth in clenched fists.

"Honey, I know the pain you're enduring. Your mama didn't know the Lord when she came to Chance Ranch. Caring turned into love before I even realized what was happening— but God's Word is clear about His children being equally yoked."

"I know," Laurel said in a tight voice.

"I'll stand beside you in prayer. If Rutlidge seeks to find the truth, it's all right there in the Bible. We'll ask the Lord to open his eyes and heart." He stroked her back. "In the end, Rutlidge has to make his own decision."

Mama reached out and held Laurel's hand. "It wasn't until I lived among your daddy and Aunt Miriam and the others that I finally saw Christianity in action. Being exposed to those whose lives were dedicated to God made me see the lack in my own heart. Maybe the reason you all went to Yosemite was for the Lord to use you to set Gabriel Rutlidge on the path of salvation."

"He talked about coming here, but that was before I told him we could only be friends. I don't know what he'll do now."

Daddy chuckled.

"It's not funny, Daddy!" she wailed.

"Oh, yes, it is." Daddy grinned at her. "Honey, no man in his right mind would let you go. He's going to pore over that Bible and show up here sooner than you think. When he does, he's bound to have a bunch of questions. Until the spiritual ones are answered, you and he aren't allowed to so much as take a walk together alone. A man who is seeking needs to keep his heart and mind on spiritual matters, and you make for one very pretty distraction."

A knock sounded on the door. Mama went to answer it. Every one of Laurel's aunts and uncles traipsed in. She knew from their expressions that they'd been told about her and Gabe.

Aunt Lovejoy bustled over and enveloped Laurel in a hug. "We love you and are so proud of you. Puttin' Jesus afore the romantic desires of yore heart—now that takes a mighty strong spirit."

"We've come to pray over Laurel," Uncle Gideon said.

Laurel looked up at her family and whispered, "I'd cherish your prayers, but Gabriel needs them more."

"God never limits our prayers," Aunt Miriam said.

"That's right. We'll pray for both of you," Uncle Titus declared.

Surrounded by their caring and wisdom, Laurel bowed her head.

fifteen

Seven days. Had it only been one week since he rode off and left Laurel? Gabe scalded his mouth with a taste of poorly brewed coffee and winced. Nothing was right. He couldn't fix a thing that tasted decent. The past two nights, he'd gotten rained on. Yosemite's beauty no longer stirred him. Loneliness swamped him. When he closed his eyes, he saw Laurel—her arms outstretched as she pressed her precious Bible into his hands. And that Bible. He couldn't ignore it.

How could one solitary object repel and yet draw a man all at the same time? Gabe told himself that he read the Good Book because it was important to Laurel. He'd promised her he'd read passages each morning and evening. Most of the time, he spent the better part of his day reading it, too—even though he didn't want to.

He'd decided to approach the New Testament as Laurel suggested: Instead of thinking of the Good Book as a collection of stories, he took it on as a way to conduct a job interview. Did he want to partner up with Jesus? Laurel told him Jesus would gladly accept him at any time.

Captain Wood rode up. "Rutledge."

"Wood." He nodded.

"What've you got there? A Bible?" The captain nodded. "Lot of power and wisdom in those pages."

Gabe carefully closed the cover and rose. "How're things going?"

The captain crossed his wrists over his saddle horn and heaved a sigh. "I'm still fighting the sheep and folks who're trying to make a fast buck by starting up businesses. Some bears raided a tent restaurant last night. The idiots left food in crates right on the ground."

"That's just begging for trouble."

Captain Wood nodded. He squinted off at Gabe's horses, then back at Gabe. "One of our mounts broke a leg in a gopher hole yesterday. I don't have any spares."

"I know a heavy-handed hint when I hear one."

"How much do you want for yours?"

"Tennessee Walker's not for sale. The pack horse it just that—a pack horse."

"I've seen him." The captain cast another assessing glance at the gelding. "He still steps lively and keeps pace with your Walker. Might not exactly be up to our usual standards, but he'll more than do in a pinch."

"Better a pack horse than shanks' mare?"

"Exactly. Too bad those Chance folks aren't still here. They had plenty of fine horseflesh, and the U.S. Cavalry has an account with them. Would have solved my problems neatly."

"They left awhile back." Gabe didn't let on that he'd been counting the days.

Captain Wood eased back in his saddle. "I know. They stopped by our headquarters in Wawona and left food behind for my men."

Thinking aloud, Gabe said, "Not that I have all that much along with me, but I won't be able to carry it all on Nessie. Can you keep some gear for me at your headquarters until I come back with another pack horse?"

"You're going to go buy another?" Captain Wood leaned forward. "I could commission you to obtain a few mounts."

The request was reasonable enough. Gabe didn't mind pitching in and helping. "Sorry. I don't know how long I'll be." Once the words exited his mouth, he could scarcely credit he'd spoken them. Still, in his heart he knew they were right. He wasn't worth a plug nickel here.

A slow smile spread across Wood's face. "Are you going after a horse, or are you chasing that comely Chance girl?"

The Bible felt strangely heavy in his hand. Gabe wanted to declare he was riding off to claim Laurel, but he couldn't. The weight in his hand didn't compare with the stone in his heart. He cleared his throat. "To be frank, I don't know what the future holds."

❧

CHANCE RANCH, the sign over the gate proclaimed. Gabe let himself onto the property, then leaned over in the saddle to make sure he latched the gate securely. For as far as he could see, and as far as he'd ridden for the past hour, strong fencing stretched across the property line. Laurel and the rest of her group hadn't let on that the family business extended to such an expansive scope.

A wry smile twisted his face. He hadn't let on that his family possessed any great wealth, either. Some things shouldn't figure into friendships and love.

Way off in the distance, he could see several rooftops. Clicking his tongue, he urged Nessie in that direction. Gabe really wanted to take her to a full gallop and reach Laurel without waiting another moment. It took all of his self-control to keep going at a sedate pace.

A huge complex came into view. A barn, a pair of sizable stables, and multiple cabins reminded him of how Laurel said all of the Chances lived together on the ranch. The place was a hive of activity. Horses frolicked in the pasture; men gathered around a corral where boys were training mounts. Chickens pecked the ground. One clump of women worked a garden while the other busily hung laundry on the clothesline.

"Stop that!" Laurel's cry from a far porch captured his attention.

Two young men Gabe didn't recognize threw punches at one another. Laurel shouted at them again, but they ignored her and continued to brawl. She lifted a nearby bucket and doused them with water. They stopped cold, and she threw down the bucket. "Both of you go home. There was no excuse for this."

Gabe sat frozen in his saddle. Was Laurel allowing other men to pay her court? The very thought sickened him. At the same time, a visceral desire to pound the daylights out of both of those boys swamped him. Laurel was his.

She made a shooing motion. "You both need to grow up. Now saddle up. I don't want to see either of you again." Her words pleased Gabe. He knew her well enough to be certain she'd meant every bit of what she said. Dressed in her yellow dress, she practically shimmered in the sunlight. As if she could feel his gaze on her, she turned toward him and lifted her hand to shade her eyes. He knew the minute she spied him. Grabbing handfuls of her skirts, she ran toward him.

Gabe set Nessie into a gallop, then pulled her to a halt and vaulted from the saddle as he neared Laurel. Arms wide open, he met her in the middle of the road. Her eyes shimmered with joy as she cried, "You came!"

Gabe wrapped his arms about her and swung her in a circle. *Let those other young bucks witness this reunion. It's time they learned Laurel belongs to me.*

Her arms wound around his neck, and she repeated breathlessly, "You came!"

Having come from a sedate home, he'd never received such a greeting. His heart swelled. "Of course I did. Nothing could keep me away."

"I take it you're Gabriel Rutlidge," someone said.

Gabe tore his gaze away from Laurel and discovered a huge clan surrounding them. He wasn't sure who'd spoken. "I am."

Laurel wiggled free of his hold and laughed nervously. "Mama, Daddy, this is Gabe. Gabe, these are my parents, Delilah and Paul Chance."

Gabe accepted Paul's outstretched hand and shook it. "Sir." He smiled at Mrs. Chance. "Ma'am, now I know where Laurel got her beautiful eyes and hair from."

As the two callers saddled up and slinked off, Laurel proceeded to introduce him to all of her aunts and uncles. Gideon, the eldest, told him, "We don't expect you to remember all of our names for a while."

"Thank you, Mr. Chance. You're a sizable family."

"None of the mister or missus stuff, either. We all answer to Chance, so you'll confuse us. We don't figure you mean any disrespect by addressing us by our given names."

"You can bunk down with us guys," Caleb offered.

"Thank you."

"Your mare's a beauty," another man said. "I'll take her to the stable and settle her in while you get situated."

Laurel patted Gabe's arm. "Uncle Bryce is itching to take a closer look at Nessie."

"We haven't had any Tennessee Walkers on the ranch," Bryce grumbled. "Can't fault a man for wanting to appreciate fine horseflesh."

"Judging from the horses everyone rode in Yosemite, I'd say the Chances know plenty about fine horseflesh." Gabe cast a look about. "And from what I see, those mounts were only a small sample of what you have on hand."

"I gotta new horse—my very own!"

"This is Perry, my brother," Laurel said.

"Congratulations, little man." Gabe reached out to shake Perry's hand. The boy gaped for a second, then puffed out his scrawny chest and shook hands.

"I cain't decide whether he's congratulatin' Perry on his horse or about bein' Laurel's brother," one aunt said to the other.

"Both," Gabe said quickly. "I'd say Perry's a very fortunate young man."

"Man's got hisself a silver tongue." The woman shook her finger at Laurel. "Gotta beware of them charmin' ones. We're gonna let him haul his gear to the boy's cabin. You 'n' me and yore mama need to finish up in the garden, else we won't have beans or salad for supper."

"Mama and I can see to that, Aunt Daisy. We're almost done. I'm sure Aunt Lovejoy could use your help with her herbs."

"Now that's a fact." A birdlike woman laced her arm through Daisy's and started to hobble off.

Gideon frowned. "Dan, Lovejoy's limping again."

"I know." Daniel grimaced. "She made me promise not to go fetch Polly or Eric."

"Polly's his daughter, and Eric is her husband," Laurel murmured. "He's a doctor, and they live in town. Polly's a healer, too."

Gabe watched as the Chance men all exchanged looks. One rocked back and forth on his heels. "Dan, you keep your word. You shouldn't fetch your daughter or son-in-law. Me? Well, I'm of the notion I need to send Tanner into town on an errand."

Caleb grinned. "No, no. I'd be happy to go, Uncle Titus. While I'm there, I just might stop in to see Polly and Eric, then I can swing by and see Greta."

April whirled around. "Stop by the kitchen before you go! I'll have food ready!"

Everyone started to disperse, and Laurel laughed. "Caleb will send back either Polly or Eric, but since neither of them can cook worth a hoot, we take mercy and send meals to them whenever someone goes to town. As much as Caleb spoke about Greta while we were gone, I presume you understand he's adept at making excuses to see her."

"This is quite some family." Gabe watched as Paxton and Caleb took his belongings off Nessie, and Bryce led the mare away.

"It is." A warm hand clamped down on his shoulder. Laurel's father nodded. "And we all take care of one another. Laurel, honey, you go back to the garden with your mama."

"Yes, Daddy." Laurel gave Gabe a shaky smile and walked away.

Paul Chance hadn't broken contact yet. He stared Gabe straight in the eyes. "Son, you're more than welcome here. Every single one of our young folks speaks highly of you. Feel free to stay as long as you want, but I'm going to have to speak frankly with you."

"I wouldn't have it any other way."

"Good. From the way my daughter raced into your arms and the way you look at her, it's plain to see feelings run deep. But that's a problem because I won't give my blessing for her to be with a man who isn't committed to walking with the Lord."

"Laurel's already made it clear to me." In the excitement of their reunion, Gabe had lost sight of that fact. Now the reality of the gulf between them loomed like an impossibility.

"She tells me you've attended church and are reading her Bible. Both are good things. I'd like to see you continue on with those. I'm not going to push or preach. None of us will. A man has to make his mind up about spiritual matters without being coaxed or coerced. Just know that if you have questions or concerns, you can come to any of us—well, anyone except Laurel."

"Are you saying I'm not to speak with her at all?"

"No. You're welcome to sit by her at the table, at devotions, and at church. If others are around, you can be, too."

Memories of the early mornings when they'd been off by themselves as she painted flashed through Gabe's mind. "When she's working on her art?"

"She and her mama often slip off together." Paul Chance didn't yield an inch. He let go and folded his arms across his chest. "I fell for my wife before she was a believer. I would have done anything to spare my daughter from being torn by the same predicament. It's too late now, but I'm going to guard her from further heartbreak as best I can."

Rooted to the ground, Gabe fought with himself. He wanted to be here; for Laurel's sake, it was best for him to leave. How could their love be wrong when they both felt it so strongly? She'd flown to him. Her own father acknowledged the depth of their feelings—but he'd also said this was breaking Laurel's heart, and Gabe remembered how Laurel had wept.

"Stay," Paul urged quietly, as if he'd sensed every thought running through Gabe's mind. "Leaving won't resolve anything. The answers you're seeking can be found. What you need is time."

"Laurel—"

A grin wide as Yosemite's meadows split across Paul's face. "Son, the fact that you're willing to put her needs above your own wants speaks volumes."

Caleb rode up. "I'm headed for town. Either of you need anything?"

Paul shook his head.

Gabe shoved his hand into his pocket and yanked out a wad of bills. He peeled off one and shoved it at Caleb. "Yeah. Laurel cherishes her Bible, and I want to give hers back to her. Could you get me a Bible of my own?"

sixteen

Gabe sat opposite Laurel at the breakfast table. Packard and Paxton bracketed him. While he turned to accept the platter of flapjacks, Pax stole the bacon from his plate. Four days ago, Laurel would have said something. Today she stayed silent and watched. Gabe had proven he could take care of himself.

Sure enough, a moment later when Paxton turned to help his little brother serve up the flapjacks, Gabe poured syrup into Paxton's coffee mug. He winked at Laurel and jerked the pitcher back to drizzle syrup on his own pancakes. A moment later, he lifted the coffeepot and filled Laurel's mug, Paxton's, Pack's, and his own. Laurel noticed it only took a small splash to fill Paxton's mug to the brim.

"Great bacon," Pax gloated as he ate a rasher. "Aunt Daisy, you sure know how to season and smoke a hog."

"Thankee." Aunt Daisy beamed at him.

"Great coffee," Gabe said after taking a big gulp.

"Yeah, our women sure can brew a fine cup," Pax agreed as he lifted his mug. He took a swig, and his eyes grew huge as he choked on it.

Gabe pounded Pax on the back. "Go down the wrong pipe?"

"Pax, how often have I told you to slow down?" Mama tsked. "Laurel, here. Pass the bacon on down to Gabe. He didn't get any."

Laurel turned to take the platter from Mama and tamped down a giggle. The sparkle in Mama's eyes proved she'd witnessed the whole exchange. Gabe grinned at them. "Thank you. Don't mind if I do have some, especially since Pax gave

Daisy's bacon such a glowing endorsement."

Pax gave Gabe a wary look. "I thought you said you only have one brother."

"That's right." Gabe helped himself to the bacon. "Stanford. He was quite a rascal in his younger days. Kept me on my toes."

"I'm sure you gave as good as you got," Pax grumbled.

"Of course I did." Gabe paused to eat another bite of bacon with relish, then added smugly, "It was a matter of honor."

Laurel and her mother exchanged a look, and both of them lost their self-control. They burst into laughter.

Gabe elbowed Pax and feigned ignorance. "What got into them?"

Pax gave him a smirk. "Who knows?"

"Hey, Pax," Cole called from the end of the table, "pass me the syrup."

"Sure." Pax lifted his coffee mug and handed it to Gabe. "Cole wants this."

Packard swiped the mug from Gabe and sent it on down. "If you two don't quit goofing off, we'll be late for church."

Cole protested, "I want syrup, not coffee!"

Kate accepted the mug, glanced down the table at Laurel, who still couldn't quell her laughter. Kate peeped in the mug, took a long drink, then snickered as she upended the mug over Cole's plate. Syrup ran out onto his pancakes.

Uncle Titus grabbed the cup and held it up in a cheering motion toward Gabe before emptying the contents onto his own plate. "No use letting good food go to waste."

"And mighty good food it is," Gabe agreed.

"Speaking of food," Tobias called over from the next table, "today is picnic day. Somebody ought to tell Gabe about the MacPhersons' dishes."

Paxton perked up and hastily cut in, "You'll have to try everything they bring, Gabe. You've eaten Lovejoy's and

Daisy's cooking. The MacPherson women come from Salt Lick Holler, too."

"I've eaten Johnna's meals in Yosemite." Gabe nodded.

"But—" Perry interrupted.

"But," Pax cut in neatly as Tanner elbowed Perry to silence him, "with us home, there's far more variety."

Laurel couldn't believe Paxton was setting Gabe up like this. The MacPhersons were good cooks—but they also had some strange notions as to what constituted food. Everyone knew to ask a discreet question or two about dishes before digging in—well, everyone except Gabe.

Beneath the table, a boot nudged her shin. Paxton gave her a sly grin. As he did so, Gabe swiped a piece of bacon off of his plate. Laurel burst out laughing again.

"What's so funny now?" Kate peered down the table at her.

"No telling," Daddy said. "Best you get finished with those giggles before we reach the sanctuary, honey."

"Yes, Daddy." Laurel blotted her mouth with her napkin.

"Oh, man," Kate moaned. "If you don't get over your giggles soon, you'd better go help in Sunday school instead of going to worship." Her face twisted into a pained expression. "Violet Greene is singing the solo today."

"There's really someone named Violet Greene?" Gabe looked to Laurel for confirmation.

As she nodded, Packard groaned loudly. "Gabe, she follows the biblical injunction to make a joyful *noise*."

"Packard Wilson Chance, if you can't say something nice," Mama began.

Everyone chimed in, "Don't say anything at all."

"I was saying something nice. I said she was following the Bible." His mouth twitched. "Besides, it's not fair to have Gabe sit in the pew and not warn him."

"It'll be like going to the opera," Gabe declared. "I listen to the lyrics, even if the music isn't always to my taste."

"You've been to an opera?" Laurel gawked at him.

"Sure." He sounded incredibly blasé as he added, "A few in New York. Once in Germany and another in Italy. Why go to Europe if you don't attend the opera?"

"I'd go to the Eiffel Tower and Rome," Caleb said.

"Of course," Gabe agreed. "In New York, I walked across the Brooklyn Bridge and climbed the Statue of Liberty, too. No use going someplace if you don't avail yourself of all it has to offer."

"Well, eat up," Daddy said as he started the platter with more flapjacks on it. "What Reliable has to offer is a big breakfast and church today."

Gabe stared across the table. Laurel's heart leapt as he said softly, "I think Reliable has plenty more to offer."

❧

Gabe stood with everyone else as the preacher gave the benediction. Other than the solo that rivaled a screeching cat, church had been downright enjoyable. He made a mental note to thank Packard for warning him about that little interlude. To Laurel's credit, she'd acted with perfect decorum during even the worst notes. As giggly as she'd been at the breakfast table, that was saying plenty.

During the sermon, Gabe used the deep purple ribbon on his Bible to mark the passage Parson Abe used. He wanted to go back and read it again. The preacher had made several interesting comments and had excellent insights. Instead of being an esoteric dissertation on theological premises, the message dealt with applicable principles. Gabe couldn't recall having ever heard such a sermon.

As a wizened old woman played the piano, folks started to leave the sanctuary. Gabe didn't like it one bit that several young men flocked toward Laurel and tried to earn her attention. To his dismay, Paul hauled him the other direction and introduced him to seemingly half of the congregation.

Exercising his manners, Gabe made small talk when what he wanted to do was plow over and yank Laurel away from those moon-eyed men.

Daniel paced over. "I spoke to the MacPhersons. I know we were due to go over to their place today, but with my Lovejoy's back acting up, they've consented to come our way."

Paul squeezed his brother's arm. "Good. I thought Lovejoy looked a tad better last evening."

"I'd rather she lie back instead of getting up, but she insists she needs sunshine and company."

Gabe folded his arms akimbo. "If you have canvas, we can take care of that."

"How?" the Chance brothers asked in unison.

"We could rig up a hammock for her."

"She does love sitting on the porch swing," Paul mused.

Daniel slapped Gabe on the back. "Let's get going!"

Gabe didn't want to leave Laurel behind. Then again, she'd be home soon. He resolved to stay glued to her side all afternoon and evening. Lovejoy deserved comfort. Helping Daniel was the least he could do.

They rode back to Chance Ranch using a shortcut through a field and over a fence. Daniel confessed, "We don't let the kids go this way. Too many rattlers and skunks through here. If your horse takes an exception to your lead, don't fight her."

"Thanks."

Gabe remembered where the ropes were kept in the stable. As he fetched them, Daniel stalked off to grab some canvas. They met in the barnyard and walked toward a nearby pasture. There, between a pair of trees, they rigged up a hammock. Daniel tested it to be sure it would sustain his wife's weight. Lying in their invention, he stacked his hands behind his head and declared, "I'm going to have to rig one of these up on my porch. Don't know why I never thought of it. My wife's going to love this."

"We could take some of that shorter length of canvas and hang a sling-style chair over a branch. That way, she could sit up to eat."

"What do you have in mind?"

"Why don't you go get your wife? I'll have it rigged by the time you carry her back here." Gabe set to work. As he finished his creation, Daniel approached, carrying his wife. Several of the young men followed behind, carrying sawhorses and planks. While Daniel settled his wife into the sling chair, the boys put up makeshift tables. In no time at all, the MacPhersons and Chances gathered together. One of the MacPherson men asked a blessing, then called out, "Okay ever'body. Dig in. We got us gracious plenty!"

Gabe swept Laurel ahead of himself in line. "Ladies first."

She smiled at him and helped herself to a spoonful of potato salad. By the time they were through the line, her plate carried a small sampling of about half of the dishes. Gabe simply figured it was due to the fact that she never seemed to have much of an appetite. He, on the other hand, took a healthy serving of just about everything.

Soon, everyone sat around on blankets in the grass and chattered as they ate. Gabe noticed how Caleb and Greta managed to carry a blanket to the very edge of the clearing and sat there alone. He envied them their privacy.

Laurel arranged her skirts and gave him a strange look. Pax scooted closer and couldn't wipe the smirk off his face. Gabe knew full well he was about to have some kind of stunt pulled on him.

"Ain't this a wondrous fine day?" one of the MacPherson women said.

Johnna nodded. "Shore is, Ma."

"Everything tastes delicious," Gabe said as he took another bite of meat.

"What've you got thar?" Johnna leaned closer.

"If it was on the table, I have some of it," Gabe confessed as he took another bite. "I'm making a pig of myself."

"You'll have to fight Pa for more of that," Johnna declared. "Ain't often we fry up a skunk."

"Skunk?" Gabe chuckled, but his chuckle died out as Paxton started whooping with delight. Turning to Laurel he raised his brows.

"Skunk," she confirmed.

seventeen

"Well." Gabe forked another bite and lifted it. "I didn't know skunk was edible. I certainly wouldn't have believed it could taste this tender."

"You're going to eat another bite?" Pax's jaw dropped.

Gabe popped the bite into his mouth. "Why not? You ought to try a taste. The flavor is excellent."

"No, thanks!"

"Don't bother tryin' to change his mind," Johnna said. "I seen bear traps looser than a stubborn man's hard head."

Laurel poked her fork into a thin strip of meat on Gabe's plate. He noticed she didn't have any of it on her plate—so he figured she was trying to give him fair warning as she said, "This is raccoon. It's one of Eunice's specialties."

"Raccoon," Gabe echoed. He covered Laurel's hand with his and bravely drew the bite up to his mouth. "Very interesting flavor. Do you have the recipe?"

"Not yet. Eunice? Gabe wants me to get the recipe for your raccoon."

"Gabe," Paxton muttered, "needs to be dragged to the nearest insane asylum."

Ulysses wolfed down a bite and shook his head. "You're missin' out, Pax. You decided what's good and right afore even testin' it out. In the end, yore cheatin' yoreself."

"My life is fine just as it is." Pax picked up a chicken leg and took a huge bite.

They spent an idyllic afternoon in the pasture. When the women started picking up all the dishes, Gabe walked over to Daniel and Lovejoy. "Lovejoy, Daniel thought you might like

140

the hammock on your porch. How does that sound to you?"

"That'd suit me fine, thankee."

"I'll carry it back for you," Gabe told Daniel.

"Obliged." Daniel stooped over his wife. "Sweetheart, I aim to lift you. It might hurt a bit."

Lovejoy reached up and wrapped her arms around his neck. "You love me, Dan'l. You'd niver hurt me."

Gabe stood to the side and silently watched as Daniel lifted his wife and carried her off. As he started untying one side of the hammock, Paul Chance began to undo the other. Gabe kept his gaze trained at the knot he'd tied so securely as he said, "I remember learning a verse when I was a kid about love casting out fear. It never made sense to me 'til now."

"Yeah," Paul agreed. "The Bible is full of wisdom. Sometimes it takes time for the truth to seep into our hearts and minds. We're so set in our ways, we can be blind to the simplest truths."

The second knot gave way under Gabe's attention. *I wouldn't have ever tried that food today had I known what it was. I wouldn't have been any different than Paxton—but tasting it without any preconceived notions led to a surprising discovery. All of the notions I've had about God—how do I know if they're true or not? The Lord these people worshiped and praised in church today isn't anything like the aloof God the pastor back home preached about.*

"This hammock was a great idea. I don't know why we never came up with it." Paul jerked at the rope and freed his side. "I suppose a fresh outlook can be a good thing sometimes."

Gabe coiled up the rope and slung the hammock over his shoulder. "Yeah. Maybe so."

❧

Laurel curled up in bed and hugged her pillow. Kate and April's whispers filled the loft of the girls' cabin, but Laurel

didn't feel like joining in on the conversation. She felt. . .
unsettled.

Home had never been like this. She'd grown up so sure all
she wanted out of life was a man to love her and to stay here,
where everything would remain comfortably the same. Only
now, the predictability of life had been blown apart.

Boys from church came by the ten days she'd been home
before Gabe arrived. Daddy had made her promise not to
close the door to a possible future with any of those boys,
and Laurel did her best to be polite—but they were all so. . .
boring. Young. Immature. None of them cared about her love
of art or asked her what she thought. Since the day Bobby
and Nestor fought and witnessed how she greeted Gabe, not
a single man in the community came to see her. That was
more than fine by her. She didn't want to mislead any of them
into believing she could ever feel more than Christian charity
toward them.

On the other hand, she had a terrible time limiting herself
to simple Christian charity toward Gabe. Her heart cried
out to be with him. Oh—they spent plenty of time together,
but everyone in the family made sure they were never alone.
Before she left for Yosemite, she adored being surrounded
by her family; now she wished they'd all go away and leave
her alone with Gabe. Only they wouldn't. Laurel knew in her
head that this was the right way to handle things. Still, deep
down inside she wanted so much more.

Chance Ranch wasn't the same, either. The youngest
members of the family weren't little children anymore. Her
aunts and uncles weren't old—but time was marching on for
them. Just as Polly had taken over most of the simple healing
and midwifery for Aunt Lovejoy, soon Laurel's generation
would assume the lion's share of responsibility for the ranch.
Laurel felt competent to do all of the necessary chores—but
what was the use of existing from day-to-day when love didn't

lift her heart? Though she was happy for Caleb and Greta, seeing them happily courting still hurt because Laurel ached to be allowed to draw closer to Gabe.

God, I don't know what to do. Gabe is all I could ever want, but he doesn't know You. Tears seeped from her tightly shut eyes. *That isn't true, Lord. I do know what to do. I know I have to put him in Your hands. I've been doing that hour by hour for weeks now. There are people who never accept You. I couldn't stand knowing Gabe was one of them.*

"Laurel?" April pulled back the covers and climbed into bed with her. She wrapped her arms around Laurel and pulled her close. "Come here."

"Scoot over," Kate added as she crept into the other side of the bed. The three of them barely fit on the mattress, but they huddled together. Kate squirmed for a minute, then handed Laurel a hanky.

"What if Gabe never makes a decision to follow the Lord?" Laurel sniffled.

"Then God will take away the love you have for him," Kate said.

"I don't believe that." April sighed. "I keep asking God to take away my love for dessert, and it hasn't gotten any easier."

Laurel let out a watery laugh. "Oh, April. I'll love you no matter what size you are."

"And you keep loving Gabe, no matter where he stands with the Lord." April patted her. "Christ loves us unconditionally. Gabe needs that same example."

"But it's not the same," Kate argued.

"Oh, what do you know? You've never been in love," April said.

"Neither have you," Kate shot back. "And I'll tell you what I do know: The Bible says we're not supposed to marry up with a man who isn't a believer. We need to help Laurel guard her heart."

"It's too late, isn't it, Laurel?"

Laurel nodded. "I do love him."

"Of course you do," Kate said. "Any dimwit could see that. What I mean is, Laurel can't act as if Gabe is going to suddenly accept Christ. She has to steel herself for the long haul. That means you and I are going to keep making pests of ourselves when Gabe is around."

"What's new about that?" Laurel asked.

"We're going to be more persistent. If you're exasperated with us, you won't be able to concentrate so much on him." Kate wiggled again like a happy puppy. "I'll tell the boys to do the same thing."

Laurel moaned. "They're already pulling all sorts of pranks on Gabe."

"Yeah, well, if Gabe really does have a change of spirit, he's going to need to be able to cope with those dopey brothers of ours. It's good training for him."

"If he can put up with it." Laurel stared up at the ceiling.

"He's obviously planning to." Kate propped up on one elbow. "Uncle Bryce talked him into having Orion service that pretty Tennessee Walker. The first pony will belong to Gabe, and the second time, Chance Ranch keeps the pony."

Laurel shot up in bed. "You're talking more than a two-year commitment!"

"Lie down and stop stealing the covers," April commanded. She jerked the quilts back up to her chin, then declared, "Gabe Rutlidge is a man of his word. He won't go back on it."

"No, he wouldn't," Laurel agreed. "He promised me he'd read the Bible twice a day, and he has."

"If you ask me, any man who can't make up his mind about the Lord or the woman he loves in two years isn't worth his weight in sawdust." Kate yawned. "Laurel, we're going to pester you and Gabe for two years. It'll be a burden, but we love you, so we'll do it. By then, if he can't get his head screwed on straight, you'll have to let him go."

April giggled. "Two years of us pestering her is liable to make her crazy enough to start frying up skunk."

"She ought to thank us. I'd never want to kiss a man who ate skunk."

"What kind of floozy do you think I am? Gabe and I haven't kissed."

"It's a good thing you haven't," April said. Without taking a breath, she continued, "What kind of man do you want to kiss, Kate?"

Kate snorted. "What difference does it make? Polly caught the doctor. Every boy in the county has chased Laurel, and when we went away, the only guy we met latched on to her. You and I don't stand a chance of ever attracting a man until we get Laurel married off."

"You're right." April swiped more of the pillow and plopped her head down on it. "That settles the matter. Gabe is going to find salvation and marry you, Laurel."

"Oh? How did you come to that conclusion?"

"Because it all makes sense. Look at the facts. In First Corinthians, it says, 'Now abideth faith, hope, charity, these three; but the greatest of these is charity.' We all have faith, and you and Gabe feel mighty charitable toward one another. That leaves hope. That's the first part. The second fact is, our heavenly Father is merciful. He'd never leave all three of us without husbands. So if you put it all together, the final fact is plain to see. Since you have to be married and out of the way before Kate or I get a crack at finding a man, we all have hope to hold fast to."

"Her logic could make Parson Abe weep in frustration," Kate mumbled.

As Laurel's cousins both slipped off to sleep, she remained wedged between them. They'd done their best to comfort her. Though their effort counted as noble, the results fell far short of the mark. Laurel had been so caught up in her own troubles, she hadn't realized they both questioned their ability to find a mate. Tucking the quilt up around all of them, she whispered the prayer they'd all agreed upon from the first night they all started living in the cabin together: "God help us all."

eighteen

"I'm sure Laurel wouldn't mind," Tobias said as he reached for the package.

"It's not for you to say." Gabe snatched the bundle from the counter in White's Emporium. "The camera is hers, as are the pictures. She ought to be the first to look at them."

"We all took photographs," Caleb said. "You know us Chances—we all share. If Laurel didn't get her nose outta joint when her brothers swiped some of her paintings to use as stationery, she certainly won't be upset if we take a peek at the pictures."

The brown paper rustled on the package as Gabe held it securely. "I'm not changing my mind."

Tobias gave him an exasperated look. "You lost your mind the day you decided to take a fancy to Laurel."

Mrs. White leaned on the counter. "Young man, don't you listen to these boys. That there is a piece of United States mail. Only person authorized to open it is the person to whom it's addressed."

"Yes, ma'am." Gabe set the package atop a good-sized crate and lifted the whole thing. He and a handful of the Chances had come to town. After dropping the crate into the buckboard and hauling the other one out, he'd head over to the doctor's office. Laurel was there, visiting with her cousin Polly.

Tobias and Caleb hefted the items they'd purchased for the ranch and tromped out to the buckboard, too. Tobias plunked down his burden, then shuffled through the mail. "Rutlidge—sure you don't wanna let us have at those pictures?

I'll trade you a letter from Boston."

Boston—it had to be from his mother or brother. "Tempting as the offer is, I'll have to decline."

"Haven't you noticed by now that on Chance Ranch, men stick together?"

"Only," Gabe retorted, "because they're honorable men, so they see eye-to-eye."

"Ouch!" Caleb slapped a hand over his heart as if he'd been shot. "Nothing like being wounded with the weapon you own."

Gabe chuckled. "Tell you what: We'll swing by and grab everyone. I'll spring for lunch at the diner, and Laurel can spread all of the pictures across the table."

"That's more like it!"

They took the largest table in the diner, but Gabe bristled when April took the seat next to Laurel. He understood why Polly sat on Laurel's other side—they missed each other and relished the opportunity to be together. But April shared the same cabin with Laurel. Surely, she could have allowed him—

"Let's see if I get it right," the waitress said as she approached the table. "Doc, Tobias, and April are going to want the pot roast. Caleb, a full pound rib eye. Laurel and Pax'll go for the blue plate—it's chicken-fried steak. Polly, it's either egg salad or corn bread and cold chicken."

"Corn bread and chicken, please."

The waitress nodded, then wrinkled her nose. "Only one I can't anticipate is you, Mr. Rutlidge."

"He's a Yankee, from Boston. Of course he'll have pot roast," Pax declared.

"Sounds good to me." Gabe set the package on the table and gave it a light push. "Laurel, here are your pictures."

Gabe suspected she would have torn open the wrapping had she been alone, but since her brother was rushing her, she took her sweet time carefully unwinding the twine and paper.

Inside the pasteboard box lay the camera and a sizable stack of photographs. Laurel removed the camera. "See, Polly? Isn't it interesting?"

"Aw, c'mon, Sis," Pax growled as he grabbed for the box.

Laurel gave him a slap on the hand. "You sit tight, Paxton. In fact, you go wash up. I don't want you touching my pictures with hands like that. Mama would have a conniption if she knew you came to the table that filthy."

Pax slinked away, and Gabe tamped down a chuckle. Laurel handled her brother with a mixture of good humor and firmness. She'd make a good mother. Just as quickly as the thought flashed through his mind, Gabe winced. He wanted her to be his wife and the mother of his children, but a wall stood between them. *And I'm the one who keeps that wall up.*

Doc turned the camera over and gave it back to Laurel. He shot Gabe a lopsided grin. "I'm always intrigued by new inventions."

"His office is full of neat stuff," Caleb attested. "Now let's look at the pictures!"

"All right. Here we go." Laurel opened the box again. One at a time, she'd remove a photograph, then tell Polly and Doc a little something about where it was taken; then it would be passed all around the table.

He loved the animation in her voice. Other than himself, Gabe knew no one else who loved Yosemite as much. He could scarcely take his gaze off of her long enough to glance at each picture.

"I took this one." April turned toward her. "May I keep it?"

"Of course."

"Then I'm keeping the one of El Capitan that I took," Caleb declared. "I've told Greta all about it, but a picture will really let her understand what the place looks like."

When the picture Gabe had taken of Laurel came around, he smiled at her and carefully slid it into his pocket. She blushed and quietly slid the photo she'd taken of him into the box.

"Hey. What's going on?" Tobias protested.

Polly pinned him with a stare. "There are one hundred pictures here. Don't tell me you're going to have a hissy fit if you don't see a couple of them."

"I need you to clear room. Food's ready."

Everyone scrambled to protect the pictures. Laurel tucked them back into the box as Doc said, "Having a camera there was a magnificent idea. Since Polly and I can't get away, it's almost as if we were able to see Yosemite for ourselves."

"Gabe traded it for some of Laurel's art," Pax said.

"I got the better end of the bargain." Gabe inclined his head toward Laurel. "That young lady has a rare talent."

"Now that I think of it, Gabe," Caleb leaned to the side so the waitress could set down his plate, "what's in those big old crates you got shipped here?"

"A variety of things." He tried to sound offhanded, but the truth of the matter was, he wanted to sort through everything alone. Most of the time, he enjoyed the camaraderie of the huge Chance clan; the past few days, he'd been feeling a need for an opportunity to be alone. "Could I please have the pepper?"

After the meal, Eric said, "I think I'll ride out to the ranch and check on Lovejoy."

"I'll come, too!" Polly hopped up from the table. "I can see Mama and Daddy and look at the rest of the photographs."

Eric chortled softly. "Translated, that means we'd better grab what we need to spend the night."

Once back at the ranch, Gabe took advantage of the fact that between chores and the pictures, everyone was busy. He slipped into the boy's cabin and read the letter from home. Everything was fine, and his mother adored Laurel's paintings. Friends had come to tea and admired the pieces so much, they wanted to acquire drawings and watercolors for themselves.

Smiling at that news, Gabe pried the lid off the first crate. Stanford had followed his instructions perfectly—the whole thing contained length after length of cloth. A rainbow of hues lay stacked there, all of them the finest Rutlidge Enterprises had to offer. Gabe turned aside to the other box. The lid groaned loudly as the nails gave way.

The contents of the box had gotten jumbled during shipping. He pushed past several spools of ribbon, drew out his best Sunday suit, and stopped cold. A small box lay nestled atop other paper-wrapped bundles. Gabe slowly reached in and opened it to find his grandmother's wedding ring. Curled inside lay a little note. "I can tell she's stolen your heart, Son. I wish you a happy life together."

The remaining bundles held another camera with a note, "Please send me pictures of the wedding!" as well as heavy white satin and lace along with a sealed envelope labeled, "To my dear daughter-in-law-to-be." Gabe slammed the lid on the box and pounded the nails in again to seal it. Every blow it took to do so matched the leaden beat of his heart.

%

As everyone took a seat for supper, Polly and Eric remained standing. Eric wound his arm around her waist and cleared his throat. "We have an announcement to make."

Laurel inhaled sharply.

"Come the first of the year, the first of the next generation is due to arrive."

After the ensuing din finally quieted down, Eric said, "We'd covet your prayers for a healthy time for Polly and the baby. There's nothing more important to us than dedicating this child back to the Lord who has blessed us with this miracle."

Uncle Gideon stood and said grace for the meal, then asked a special blessing for Eric, Polly, and the baby. Touched by the absolute sweetness of the news and the presence of the Lord, Laurel wiped her eyes as she lifted her head.

Gabe stared at her. A tiny muscle in his jaw twitched. Throughout supper, he barely said a word. As it was her turn to dry the dishes, Laurel couldn't keep track of him after supper, and he didn't show up when the whole family gathered for bedtime devotions.

Laurel couldn't sleep. Long after April and Kate went to bed, she stayed up. By the light of a single lamp, she cut tiny garments out of soft white cotton and started stitching them. Sewing and art always calmed her—only tonight, it didn't work.

She'd seen the bleakness in Gabe's eyes at supper.

Her Bible sat open on the table to the Fifty-first Psalm. Each day, she'd read the same psalm Gabe was supposed to be reading. This one, though, she knew was aimed at her. Long ago, she'd memorized the passage starting at the tenth verse. Now it pierced her heart with every stitch she took:

> Create in me a clean heart, O God;
> and renew a right spirit within me.
> Cast me not away from thy presence;
> and take not thy holy spirit from me.
> Restore unto me the joy of thy salvation;
> and uphold me with thy free spirit.

Laurel knew she'd done the right thing by telling Gabe their relationship wasn't acceptable in the sight of God. The truth of the matter was, she'd still been in the wrong. Instead of releasing her dreams and desires and letting the Lord direct her path, she'd had a stubborn spirit. Facing that fact struck her to the depths of her soul.

Lord, I was wrong. Help me to remember the joy of my salvation and give me the strength to follow Your will. You'll have to do this work in my heart and soul, Father. I won't ever to be ready to be a good wife and mother if I don't keep You first in my life. It hurts to let go, Lord. Please help me.

Tears wet the little gown in her lap.

nineteen

Gabe sat out on a split rail fence, staring up at the sky. He'd walked away from the supper table, but he couldn't escape the sight of the tears glistening in Laurel's eyes. She'd make a wonderful wife and spectacular mother—but he denied her both of those dreams. Oh, she'd smiled at him, a bittersweet smile that reflected how much she longed to be his wife and the mother of his babies. He knew she'd not given her heart lightly when they fell in love. *But what kind of man am I to bind her heart and make her settle for nothing in return?*

"Sittin' on the fence, huh?"

Gabe glanced over his shoulder. Paul Chance stood a few yards away. "Are you speaking literally or figuratively?"

"Take it whichever way you choose."

Smacking his hand down on the fence, Gabe offered a silent invitation to join him.

Paul sauntered over and shot Gabe a grin. "We're both big men and some of these slats are brittle. Might break if we put too big of a burden on 'em." After banging against the fence, he hitched up beside Gabe. "I've spent my share of time sitting off on my own, staring off into the distance, and trying to settle matters."

"Is that so?"

"Yup. Fact is, I didn't know you were out here. I came to do some thinking and praying. Seems you like the same spot I do."

Gabe started into motion to leave, but Paul stilled him. "I reckon since you were the subject of my thoughts and prayers, maybe you're meant to stay."

"You were thinking and praying for me?"

Paul nodded. "Of course I am. Son, you're a fine man—intelligent, hardworking, and kind. I've put myself square in front of what you want so badly, but you've respected my limits instead of resenting me."

"You've stood on your principles, and I honor that. I can't help wondering, though, whether there's room for compromise. If I vow to take Laurel to church each week, read the Bible, and pray, isn't that enough?"

"No," Paul said baldly. "Marriage blends two souls into one, but if you don't belong to the Lord, that bond can't be what it was meant to be. A man is the spiritual head of a home. If your head and heart aren't right with God, how can my daughter and grandchildren rely on your decisions and leadership?"

Gabe gritted his molars and shifted his weight.

"Son, I'm not pushing you to make any decisions. Having you here is a joy. Every last Chance on this ranch likes and cares for you. When you first arrived, I told you to take all the time you need. What I am going to say is, I think you're focusing on the wrong thing. Instead of trying to patch up a way you and Laurel can wed, you need to concentrate on the restlessness you feel deep inside."

"I never said I was restless."

"Didn't need to. You left your family. Wandered all over Yosemite on your lonesome. Stare off into the fire during devotions. Trust me—I've got brothers, sons, and nephews. I've seen the same struggle more than a dozen times. Only one thing solves it."

Gabe gave him a crooked smile. "Laurel sort of said the same thing. She said man was made with a void only God fills—that's why Adam walked with God in the Garden of Eden."

"Yep. I'm sure she mentioned sin separates us from God.

Being without the Father leaves us restless. We keep trying to find something to fill up the empty spot, but nothing works."

"So your advice is to pay attention to myself instead of Laurel?"

"Did you notice how I tested the fence before I sat on it?"

"Yeah." Gabe wondered why he'd asked such a bizarre question.

"That's because my brothers and I put up this fence a long time ago. It was solid as could be. Able to carry a burden and do the job. But time passes. Weathering and wear take their toll. What once was reliable can crumble under a heavy burden."

Gabe listened. He wasn't sure where this was going.

"Son, men build fences for a reason. I'm not talking about a fence like the one we're sitting on. Inside, men build fences so they feel strong and capable of handling everything on our own. We're prideful, and keeping busy gives us a sense of accomplishment. Only in the dead quiet of night is the truth clear: Those fences only serve to keep out God and the ones we love. In the end, life wears us down. Either we have the Lord to rely on, or we fall apart."

"I've known prideful Christian men."

"I wouldn't dream to deny that." Paul chuckled. "We still sin, but the good news is that we're granted forgiveness when we ask for it. Just talk to Eric. Fine Christian. Came here to Reliable wanting to serve the Lord with his doctoring. His pride sure got bruised when Polly and Lovejoy kept treating folks and delivering the babies. When he finally set aside that pride, God did a mighty work. Now he and Polly heal the sick and are expecting a miracle of their own. It wasn't until Eric yielded that God moved in, though."

Laurel's father pushed off the fence. "I didn't come here to preach. I could tell you stories all night, but in the end, each man has to wrestle with his own heart. If you want someone to pray with you or answer questions, I'm available—so are any of my brothers or Parson Abe. It's the biggest decision any of us makes, so consider carefully. I respect that you've not made any pretenses or snap judgments."

"Thank you." Gabe stayed on the fence and watched Paul walk off. In a very short conversation, Laurel's father had managed to say quite a bit. Gabe needed time to think things through.

He wasn't wrong. I've been concentrating so much on finding a way to have Laurel be mine, I've ignored the root of the problem.

Laurel had urged him to read the scriptures as a means to get to know Christ. Gabe started thinking of the Gospels he'd read, and Christ's character traits seemed like such an unlikely combination. For being such a charismatic leader, Jesus had been astonishingly humble. He'd possessed undeniable power—the miracles He wrought testified to that—but He used His abilities only to serve. Compassion and mercy flowed from Him, yet He'd also stood firm for His convictions.

Gabe trudged back toward the boys' cabin. Lying in the dark, he couldn't stop the confusing whirl of thoughts. Rustling made him roll over. Tobias was sitting on the edge of his own bed, leaning across the space between their bunks.

"Can't sleep?" Gabe asked.

"Neither can you." Tobias drummed his fingers on his knee, then said, "You left your Bible open on your bunk this morning. I wondered all day whether you did it on purpose so someone would ask if you wanted to discuss what you'd read."

Gabe sat up. "I don't recall leaving it open."

Tanner grumbled from the other side of the cabin, "Take it outside. Some of us wanna get some shut-eye."

"No pressure. Just an offer." Tobias didn't move at all.

Gabe shrugged into his shirt. As they exited the cabin, he

noticed Tobias had grabbed the Bible.

"Barn's probably the best place for us to go," Tobias ventured. "We can light a lantern."

Soon they sat on bales of hay that formed a V by the post from which a lantern hung. Tobias bowed his head. Gabe assumed he was praying, so he sat quietly. After a few moments, he flipped through the Bible, and the pages parted where Gabe had placed the ribbon that morning.

"I notice you have the ribbon and Laurel's picture as a bookmark in there," Tobias said.

"I promised Laurel I'd read a Psalm each morning and the New Testament at night." He didn't mention how he'd used the picture as his bookmark so Laurel's face was the last thing he saw each night. "I haven't gotten to tonight's stuff yet."

"What part of the New Testament are you reading?"

"I started at the beginning. I've read Matthew, Mark, and Luke. I got started in John last night. Jesus told Nicodemus that he had to be born again. I stopped reading when I hit John 3:16. It was sort of like being a kid in Sunday school—I remember memorizing that verse."

Tobias grinned. "I remember that one, too. Dad almost choked to death on the popcorn he was eating when I recited it for him because I said God so loved the world, he gave His only *forgotten* Son."

Gabe chuckled. "My brother, Stanford, thought the Israelites all had to eat *eleven* bread."

"It's easy to see how kids get stuff like that mixed up. Fact of the matter is, I think adults also get mixed up. We think we have a grasp of what the Bible or preacher says, but when it comes to getting through life, we don't always have the facts straight."

"Until you folks came to Yosemite, I thought I had a handle on everything."

"Do you?"

Gabe sat in silence. Finally he shrugged. "Part of me wants to say I do. The other part is calling me a liar."

"What's right in your life?" Tobias eased into a more comfortable position.

"My mom and brother are fine. I've got more than enough money to see me through. I've got free rein in Yosemite."

"Now the other side of the coin—what's not right?"

Gabe shifted uncomfortably. "Laurel. I'm breaking her heart, and it's killing me. Her dad told me tonight to stop paying attention to her feelings and to focus on myself. I'm trying, but it's hard. He said the restlessness I feel is because I lack peace in my soul."

"Do his words ring true to you?"

"I never even paid attention to my soul until Laurel pointed out that I lacked any personal commitment. Being around you Chances—I see you're different."

"Is it a difference that you want for yourself?"

Gabe leaned forward and rested his elbows on his knees. "I've read the Bible before—it was like a big collection of stories. Sort of like mythology and fairy tales. In my head, I figured they were basically true. Now I'm reading it with the intent of figuring out if Jesus is someone I'd want as a partner."

Tobias didn't say anything.

Gabe rested his chin on his palm. "To begin with, I'm not sure I want a partner. I like controlling my own life. So far I've done a good job of it. It may sound proud, but I've been honest and moral. The other thing is, I don't cotton to the notion of having God tell me what to do."

"If you're already living an honest, moral life, why would you expect God to direct you to do something outside of what your heart would lead you to do?"

Gabe let out a rueful chuckle. "Can't say I ever thought of it like that."

Tobias hitched a shoulder. "To take it a step further, we're only flesh and blood. We slip up. There are times we don't make the right choices. Christians still sin. When that's the case, I figure we deserve to be chastened, to confess, and to ask for forgiveness. God grants that grace to us through the blood of Jesus."

"But what kind of partnership is that? Jesus is perfect, but He pays the price. Man messes up and keeps getting the benefits."

"It's the most lopsided deal of all time. The truth is, we have a choice: We can be proud and live life on our own, or we can yield and accept."

"No in-between ground, huh?"

"Nope." Tobias shook his head. "We have nothing to bargain with. Man can't earn his way into eternity."

"That woman at church last Sunday testified all about feeling God calling her. What if He's not calling me? I don't hear or feel anything."

"The Holy Spirit works in different ways. Some people make their decision to follow God based on an emotional tug. Me?" Tobias spread his hands wide. "Practicality always wins out. I came to the point where I realized I had no call to be proud—Christ did more than I ever could. For me, in my life, I wanted Him to take charge and lead the way."

"I can't believe you ever did anything very sinful."

Tobias rubbed the toe of his boot on the calf of his jeans. "Growing up in a family like mine, I had plenty of people keeping an eye on me. I've never gotten drunk, had relations with a woman, or murdered someone. But I've been mean to my brothers and cousins. I've shaded the truth and shirked my chores."

Gabe made a scoffing sound. "Those are ordinary things. Everyone does them."

"They're still sins." Tobias looked him in the eyes. "Everyone does them because everyone sins. We all do. It's why we're all separated from God. Man tries to justify those actions by pointing to the fact that other wrongs are worse—but sin is sin."

"I've always figured humans are entitled to slip up. I didn't think of it as sin."

"Where do you draw the line? When is it merely a 'slip up' and when is it a sin? First John says, 'If we say that we have no sin, we deceive ourselves, and the truth is not in us. If we confess our sins, he is faithful and just to forgive us our sins, and to cleanse us from all unrighteousness.'"

Gabe winced. "That doesn't pull any punches. It condemns me because any wrong I've done is sin."

"No matter how 'good' we are, we still fail. God loves us and sent Christ to redeem us."

Gabe sat in silence. Memories assailed him. All along, he'd considered himself an upstanding man; but by this measuring stick, he was nothing but a sinner. He buried his face in his hands.

Tobias reached over and took the Bible. He read aloud the first verses from the Fifty-first Psalm that Gabe had read that morning. " 'Have mercy upon me, O God, according to thy lovingkindness: according unto the multitude of thy tender mercies blot out my transgressions. Wash me throughly from mine iniquity, and cleanse me from my sin. For I acknowledge my transgressions: and my sin is ever before me.' " He paused, then quietly added, "God's forgiveness is there. All you have to do is confess and ask Him into your life."

Gabe nodded. "I need to do that."

They knelt by the bales of hay. Tobias wrapped his arm around Gabe's shoulders. "Do as the verse said. Confess that you've been a sinner and claim salvation through the merciful blood of Christ."

For all the times he'd bowed his head, Gabe had never felt like this. Throat tight, heart pounding, he rasped, "God, I used to think I was good enough; but I'm not. My heart was full of pride, and I've sinned." Tears seeped from his tightly shut eyes, and his voice died out.

Tobias squeezed him.

"I'm asking You, Lord, to forgive me. It's only through Jesus' death on the cross that I can beg that of you. Change me, God. Help me be the man You would have me be. Amen."

≈

Gabe couldn't wait. He strode across the barnyard and rapped on the door.

"Just a minute," a sleep-husky voice called. A few seconds later that same person grumbled, "This better be important."

Gabe grinned as Paul Chance opened the door. "Yeah, it's important. I know you've been praying for me. Thought you might want to move your attention to a different soul who's lost since I'm found."

Paul let out a whoop and yanked him inside. " 'Lilah!"

Delilah knotted the sash of her robe as she came into view. "What's wrong?"

"Not a thing." Paul wrapped his arm around Gabe's shoulder and pulled him close. "Tell her, son."

"I asked Christ into my heart tonight."

Laurel's mother burst into tears as she dashed across the room and enfolded him into a hug. "How wondrous!"

"It is," Gabe agreed. "I figure I have a lot to learn about living as a man of God. I was hoping I could ask for some guidance."

"I'm honored you've asked. I'd be happy to disciple you."

Delilah wiped her eyes. "You couldn't ask a better man. I've been blessed to have Paul as my husband."

"Speaking of husbands. . ." Gabe straightened his shoulders.

"I'd like to ask the two of you to allow me the honor of being Laurel's husband."

Paul and Delilah exchanged a look Gabe couldn't interpret. Paul then turned to him and said, "There's a problem."

twenty

"Do you know what's going on?" Kate asked Laurel as they prepared breakfast.

"No." Laurel cast a worried look through the window, over at the bend in the creek. All of the Chance adults sat in a circle there. They'd called a meeting.

"This is Caleb's first time to get to vote," April said. "As soon as they're done, I'll see if I can worm any information out of him. I know just how to convince my brother to talk." She waggled her brows and set aside a sticky bun.

Laurel didn't laugh. She couldn't. Gabe sat in the circle with her parents, aunts, and uncles. His presence at that meeting constituted a complete departure from family tradition.

"This is so odd," Kate said as she cracked eggs into a bowl. "Tobias is strutting around today with the biggest smile you ever saw, but he's not saying a word. He's never like that."

"What do you mean? Tobias hardly ever says much," April disagreed.

"Well, he's only three months from his twenty-first birthday. I figured he'd be put out that they didn't ask him to be part of the vote."

Laurel dropped the rasher of bacon she'd lifted to turn. "They're voting? On what?"

"I don't know. I just assumed they were voting." April grimaced. "I shouldn't have said anything—not when they asked Gabe to be there. Oh. Wow! Caleb's hot about something."

Laurel and Kate gawked out the window and watched as Caleb stood, gestured emphatically, and stalked off. A few moments later, he rode away.

"Oh! The bacon's burning!" Kate cried.

Laurel ran back over and hastily saved most of it. A few rashers were like strips of black leather. She dumped them into the swill bucket for the hogs as April and Kate both opened the doors to get rid of the smoke. Tears ran down Laurel's cheeks. She hoped her cousins would attribute them to the smoke.

Lord, prepare my heart for what's going to happen. I'm so afraid. They're going to send Gabe away. I put this all in Your hands last night, but it's so hard to leave it there.

"Laurel?" Gabe's voice stopped her cold. "I'd like to speak with you."

"Let me wash my hands." She kept her back to him and tried to gather her courage. After washing up and taking off her apron, she turned around.

Gabe held out his hand. "Let's go for a walk."

She closed her eyes to block out the sight of that potent temptation. "I can't. You know I'm not allowed to be alone with you."

He drew closer, and his hand closed around hers. "Your father gave us permission. Come on."

She couldn't bear to look up into the face of the man she still loved. Laurel dipped her head and nodded. He squeezed her hand and led her out the back door. As she passed by her cousins, April silently shoved a hanky into her hand.

Gabe didn't say anything as they walked along the dusty path toward a stand of trees. Once under their canopy, he halted and leaned back into one of them. Reaching down, he took Laurel's other hand in his. "I need to tell you something."

Laurel braced herself.

"Look at me," he commanded in a gruff tone.

Trying her hardest to look composed, Laurel tilted her head back.

"Much better," he said. The smile on his face took her off guard. "I asked Christ to be my Lord and Master last night."

It took a moment for his words to sink in. When they did, Laurel squealed his name in delight.

He chortled and pulled her close. Hugging her, he whispered into her hair, "Princess, I wouldn't have ever known I needed Him if you hadn't taken a stand."

"I'm so happy for you."

He tipped her face up to his. "I'm happy for me, too. But there's something else. I'm happy for *us*. Your father gave us his blessing."

Laurel burst into tears.

Gabe clasped her to his chest as she soaked the hanky and his shirt. Finally, he said, "I'd hoped that would make you happy."

"It does." She sniffled. "You don't know how much it does. Last night, I decided I needed to trust God instead of telling Him what I wanted. Today, when they had the meeting, I was afraid they were going to tell you to leave."

"You can't get rid of me that easily." He stroked her cheek. "We had to work out a little problem, though."

Laurel's heart skipped a beat.

"I'll get to that in a minute." He smiled at her tenderly. "I love you, Laurel."

Finally free to confess it, she whispered, "I love you, too, Gabriel."

Gabe pulled her out to a small patch of sunlight, lifted her by her waist, and spun her around as he let out a laugh. Once he set her down, he went down on one knee. "Laurel, my love, will you marry me?"

"Yes!" She couldn't believe he'd asked. Through tear-sheened eyes, she watched as he drew a ring from his pocket.

"This was my grandmother's ring. I'd like you to wear it as a symbol of our pledge to wed."

"Gabe, I'm honored."

"Rutlidge tradition holds that I grace your hand with an additional ring on the day we marry." He slid it onto her finger and rose. "Now about that little problem."

"Nothing could be a problem on a day like today."

"Yes, it could." He crooked a brow. "I've been informed that before you all left for Yosemite, it was with the understanding that no one would get married until autumn of next year."

"Oh, no." Laurel covered her mouth in horror as she recalled the agreement. She hung her head. "I forgot all about that. We all thought it was just a way to make Caleb and Greta wait awhile longer. I'm sorry, Gabe. I had no right to make a promise when I wasn't speaking just for myself."

He chuckled. "I'm going to have to plead guilty to the same crime."

"There's nothing funny about this." She looked up at him.

"Yes, there is. Or at least I hope you'll see it that way. They took a vote. Your parents, aunts, uncles, Polly, Eric, and Caleb all agreed to release you and Caleb from that pledge on one condition."

"What?"

"Actually, it's two conditions." Gabe's eyes sparkled.

"Don't you dare keep me wondering. Tell me!"

"First, Greta has to accept Caleb's proposal."

Laurel let out a laugh. "I'm sure she will."

"The other thing—well, Caleb and I made a pledge." He paused. "I spoke for both of us without consulting you. I won't make a practice of it, Laurel, but under the circumstances, I hope you'll understand. I know women are touchy about things like this."

She couldn't stand it. "Just tell me."

"Caleb and I told them if we could get married in three weeks, we'd talk you girls into a double wedding."

"Three weeks!" she gasped.

"And I thought you were going to be upset about a double wedding."

"Why would I? We've told you time and again, Chances share."

"You won't be a Chance much longer, princess." He pulled her close and dipped his head. "But right about now, how about if we share a kiss?"

❧

"Where's my shirt?" Gabe looked around the cabin in a panic. "I can't find my shirt!"

"It's gotta be around here," Caleb muttered as he yanked a comb through his hair.

"Caleb, I have your shirt here," Miriam called from the other side of the door.

Gabe and Caleb both stared at the shirt Caleb was wearing and burst out laughing. Gabe opened the door, grabbed the shirt, and said, "Thanks!" as he shut it again. As he shrugged into the freshly-ironed shirt, he said, "You Chances—your policy for sharing is going to make me crazy."

"Don't you dare let on about this." Caleb craned his neck as he knotted his tie. "We'd never hear the end of it—not after the way we've teased the women the past three weeks."

The day he'd proposed, Gabe had given Laurel the bridal satin and lace. He'd also given the crate with all the other fabric to her family. They'd been delighted with the material and each claimed a length for a dress to wear to the wedding. Since then, the women had spent every moment they could in the girls' cabin. Discussions about sewing, the plans for the wedding, and countless details filled their conversation. The men all sat back and found the whole thing amusing.

Caleb announced just one week into the preparations, "I don't know what the fuss is all about. Greta's seen me in dusty, ripped jeans, and I've seen her looking like a drowned rat after a downpour. Our marriage would be just as strong if I dragged her to the altar this Sunday and we said our 'I do's.'"

Gabe counted himself fortunate that he'd not opened his mouth. Every woman on the ranch scolded Caleb. He'd been called "unromantic," and they'd listed all of the essential preparations that included everything from gowns to trousseaus, flowers, cakes, and any number of other details. Gabe nodded solemnly, as if those things actually mattered. The way Laurel beamed at him made him feel dishonest, so he leaned over and confessed, "Princess, I want our wedding day to be all you ever dreamed of. None of this matters to me—but I know it's important to you."

Only now, as he and Caleb got ready to go to the church, did Gabe realize he and Caleb were both less than collected and calm. He'd never tell a soul that he'd crammed his right foot into his left shoe. Finally dressed, combed, and ready, he turned to Caleb. "Well, let's get this done."

＆

Polly met Laurel's wagon at the church. "I pinned the boutonnieres on the grooms' lapels after they both tried and managed to stab themselves."

Daddy carried Laurel into the back of the church so her hem wouldn't get dusty. Before setting her on her feet, he whispered, "Your mama and I prayed for the right man for you. We're sure God's listened to our prayers."

"Thank you, Daddy."

Greta and her family arrived. Soon the pianist started the processional, and Greta's sisters and Laurel's cousins walked in to serve as bridesmaids. Rather than have the "Bridal March" played twice, Greta and Laurel had decided to have their fathers escort them down the side aisles of the church simultaneously. Clutching her flowers and her father's arm, Laurel walked along as if in a dream.

Last night, after telling her he loved her, Gabe had promised, "I'll meet you in the middle tomorrow."

Now he did just that. Daddy led her around the edge, up to the middle of the front of the church and placed her hand in Gabriel's. They spoke their sacred vows and shared communion. Parson Abe invited Gabe to greet his bride. Laurel shivered in anticipation as Gabe reached for the edge of her veil. Their kiss held the promise of a blessed future.

Later, as they all ate at the wedding feast, someone asked, "Are you going on a honeymoon?"

Gabe nodded. "I'm taking my bride to Wawona."

Paxton laughed. "I think that's called returning to the scene of the crime."

Johnna poked him. "You be nice. Yosemite's beautiful. I'll bet nothin's purdier than Bridal Veil in the early autumn."

Gabe turned to Laurel and dipped his head. He whispered in her ear, "Almost nothing. I've discovered a different bridal veil on a unique beauty. She stole my heart."

Laurel turned toward him. "Heart and soul—now we can be one."

"Whooo-ooo-ie. Lookit the lovebirds," one of the Mac-Phersons shouted out. "Go on, give yore gal a kiss."

"Don't mind if I do," Caleb said loudly.

Gabe reached up and kissed his fingertips as Laurel did the same. Their fingers then met in the middle as their laughter carried the anticipation of many years of happiness.

A Letter To Our Readers

Dear Reader:

In order that we might better contribute to your reading enjoyment, we would appreciate your taking a few minutes to respond to the following questions. We welcome your comments and read each form and letter we receive. When completed, please return to the following:

Fiction Editor
Heartsong Presents
PO Box 719
Uhrichsville, Ohio 44683

1. Did you enjoy reading *Bridal Veil* by Cathy Marie Hake?
   ❑ Very much! I would like to see more books by this author!
   ❑ Moderately. I would have enjoyed it more if

   _____

   _____

   _____

2. Are you a member of **Heartsong Presents**? ❑ Yes ❑ No
   If no, where did you purchase this book? _____

   _____

3. How would you rate, on a scale from 1 (poor) to 5 (superior), the cover design? _____

4. On a scale from 1 (poor) to 10 (superior), please rate the following elements.

   ____ Heroine   ____ Plot
   ____ Hero   ____ Inspirational theme
   ____ Setting   ____ Secondary characters

5. These characters were special because? _____

_____

_____

6. How has this book inspired your life? _____

_____

_____

7. What settings would you like to see covered in future
   Heartsong Presents books? _____

_____

_____

8. What are some inspirational themes you would like to see
   treated in future books? _____

_____

_____

9. Would you be interested in reading other **Heartsong
   Presents** titles? ❑ Yes ❑ No

10. Please check your age range:
    ❑ Under 18   ❑ 18-24
    ❑ 25-34   ❑ 35-45
    ❑ 46-55   ❑ Over 55

Name _____

Occupation _____

Address _____

City, State, Zip _____

Nebraska Legacy

4 stories in 1

American settlers become husbands in the most unusual of circumstances.

Titles by author DiAnn Mills include: *Mail Order Husband, Temporary Husband, Kiowa Husband,* and *Renegade Husband.*

Historical, paperback, 480 pages, 5³⁄₁₆" x 8"

_____

Please send me _____ copies of *Nebraska Legacy*. I am enclosing $6.97 for each.
(Please add $2.00 to cover postage and handling per order. OH add 7% tax.)
Send check or money order, no cash or C.O.D.s, please.

Name_____

Address_____

City, State, Zip _____

To place a credit card order, call 1-740-922-7280.
Send to: Heartsong Presents Readers' Service, PO Box 721, Uhrichsville, OH 44683

Heart♥ong

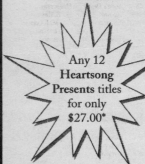

Presents

HEARTSONG
PRESENTS

If you love Christian romance...

You'll love Heartsong Presents' inspiring and faith-filled romances by today's very best Christian authors...DiAnn Mills, Wanda E. Brunstetter, and Yvonne Lehman, to mention a few!

When you join Heartsong Presents, you'll enjoy four brand-new, mass market, 176-page books—two contemporary and two historical—that will build you up in your faith when you discover God's role in every relationship you read about!

Imagine...four new romances every four weeks—with men and women like you who long to meet the one God has chosen as the love of their lives...all for the low price of $10.99 postpaid.

To join, simply visit www.heartsong presents.com or complete the coupon below and mail it to the address provided.

$10.99

Mass Market 176 Pages

YES! Sign me up for Heartsong!

NEW MEMBERSHIPS WILL BE SHIPPED IMMEDIATELY!
Send no money now. We'll bill you only $10.99 postpaid with your first shipment of four books. Or for faster action, call 1-740-922-7280.

NAME _____

ADDRESS_____

CITY_____ STATE _____ ZIP _____

MAIL TO: HEARTSONG PRESENTS, P.O. Box 721, Uhrichsville, Ohio 44683
or sign up at **WWW.HEARTSONGPRESENTS.COM**